The author has had the opportunity of working in Legal work, Social work and Education both privately and publicly, The skills she has acquired have allowed and encouraged her to act as an advocate for those who have no voice or are unable to communicate their voice. The background has enabled her to portray to the reader just how easy it is for the elderly, and the venerable, to be duped by those closest to them that they believe they can trust. Their vulnerability allows unscrupulous individuals, or groups, to take advantage of them, their homes, possessions, their memories and their peace of mind.

I dedicate this book to all those who believe in justice and peace of mind. And, to all those who believe duplicity' is just a word like 'hedonist' I say take heed for God plays debts without money!

And my family for persevering with me for two years whilst writing this book.

Sally Anne Burberry

PURELY FOR THE MONEY AND NOT A LITTLE LOVE

AUSTIN MACAULEY PUBLISHERS™
LONDON • CAMBRIDGE • NEW YORK • SHARJAH

Copyright © Sally Anne Burberry 2023

The right of Sally Anne Burberry to be identified as author of this work has been asserted by the author in accordance with sections 77 and 78 of the Copyright, Designs and Patents Act 1988.

All rights reserved. No part of this publication may be reproduced, stored in a retrieval system, or transmitted in any form or by any means, electronic, mechanical, photocopying, recording, or otherwise, without the prior permission of the publishers.

Any person who commits any unauthorised act in relation to this publication may be liable to criminal prosecution and civil claims for damages.

This is a work of fiction. Names, characters, businesses, places, events, locales, and incidents are either the products of the author's imagination or used in a fictitious manner. Any resemblance to actual persons, living or dead, or actual events is purely coincidental.

A CIP catalogue record for this title is available from the British Library.

ISBN 9781398498433 (Paperback)
ISBN 9781398498440 (ePub e-book)

www.austinmacauley.com

First Published 2023
Austin Macauley Publishers Ltd®
1 Canada Square
Canary Wharf
London
E14 5AA

I would like to thank Daniel Hibble for letting me use
The Bell at Kersey for the front cover of the book

Chapter 1

There was a time when they were a family to be revered. Not so now! Where to begin, right from the beginning or someway halfway between? Perhaps halfway between with a pinch of what's to come!

A family of four with their roots in London and three hearts in Constable Country with its beautiful scenery, idyllic waters, a mill and much, much more. Randall and Hannah had one property in London and their holiday home in Suffolk. Their eldest, Sophie, lived in Suffolk and was able to look after their holiday home all week until Randall and Hannah could get up at weekends and on every holiday that they could manage. They loved their little country nest. As the next few years rolled on they both travelled backwards and forwards to work and to see their families and venture further into Suffolk and Norfolk visiting stately homes; Randall loved history and paintings and Hannah loved all the furnishings and chandeliers.

Randall had a brief taste of the good life years ago when London was bombed during the blitz. He and other children were sent into the country for safety. He had been sent to a large country estate run by two elderly spinsters. He spoke of how the two sisters would always dress for dinner in evening gowns and their Ermine stoles. It was the first time he had been given pyjamas and a bed of his own. The children all slept in a large dormitory. He was later to recognise what he wanted out of life, a life much better than he had. He had an abundance of love from his parents and siblings but his later experiences made him determined to have a better lifestyle.

Randall had been too young to join his brothers in the forces, never the less; he was not immune to the horrors of war and what it did to people. When trying to describe to Sophie what it was like he would get upset and explain what it was to be in your home enjoying a meal and then having to rush to an air raid shelter for safety. He explained that sometimes you would come out of the shelter and find that your friends' house had been bombed and, if lucky, they had been in the shelter with him, others, were not so lucky and hadn't made it to the shelter. There were times when Randall would break down in tears at what he had seen. He was particularly upset when, at the age of 14 years old, he had been walking home and looked up into a tree at what he thought at first was a child's doll, he then saw that it wasn't a doll but a baby that had been blown up into the tree during the bombing! His war, through the eyes of a teenager, was to have a lasting impact on him. No longer did he want to live in fear, and poverty and without all those things that we now take for granted; life, liberty, freedom of speech, and freedom to our own religion.

Randall's parents were poor but there was always a lot of love. He had many brothers and sisters, most of whom were older than him, and their father taught them all to box. They were all, as they grew older, staunch Union Men and two of them were Union Representatives. Choosing which party you were going to vote for wasn't really an option, all were very much working class with no opportunity for management positions, so it had to be labour! This family were just like any other in the East End of London. Their life and upbringing made them who they were!

The eldest brother was the first to move away from London and, later, a few of their nephews and nieces. Sophie was one of them.

Sophie had recently divorced and had to pick up more work to cover the debts she'd been left with. The last four months after the divorce found that half the mortgage hadn't been paid and obviously had to be paid back before she lost the house. Within 18 months all the debts had been paid and a little had been put back into the savings account for "a rainy day"! Sophie was without a car, she couldn't afford one now that she was divorced and a single mother so Randall gave her his old one and it had been a Godsend to her for many years. He "couldn't get much on it, even as a trade in", and Sophie would need a car to get her shopping and keep an eye on their holiday home for Randall and Hannah he said.

Sophie made sure that their little home was always safe and warm and with plenty of ready food, especially in the snowy days, to make sure they didn't have to rush out to buy essentials and could rest and relax at the weekends until Randall had to return to London on Sunday afternoons for work the following day. Every holiday was spent in their little country residence. They were very proud of their home and furnished it to high standards and "cosyness". Christmas was a special time when they could see their family but also friends and neighbours! Within the county and just beyond lived Hannah's sister-in-law and niece and Randall's sister and her family.

Randall was very unfortunate in starting to experience health issues, which were identified as cancer. It was unexpected and meant that many changes to their lives had to take place. Randall had to have an operation that could have very serious effects on his work and his life. Before long Randall had to retire from his job on medical grounds. From now on, after his cancer operation, he wanted to get plenty of rest and relaxation, away from the smoke and the rush and bustle, he was so pleased that he and Hannah had decided to buy there own small little place with just a little land to grow his "fruit and vegetables", would be just enough to keep him occupied. Idyllic! He was glad that they had found somewhere before his cancer had been diagnosed. Hannah missed London from time to time as she had always been a "town girl" but, before long, she recognised the need for a different pace of life to give them both valuable time together because there was always the chance that cancer would come back. Randall kept the outside neat and tidy and Hannah kept the inside. She had never really known any other life other than domestic as she had always had to help her mother look after the house and help look after her younger siblings.

Hannah's father was very strict with his sons but not so with his daughters. They all lived in a big house owned by The Crown (The Queen). Hannah's father was "the middle man" who bought and sold a large variety of provisions from the wholesalers to the retailers. Attached to the house was a large warehouse and this enabled Hannah's father to store the butter, bacon, cheeses and other items the retailers might request. The weighing scales for all the merchandise were huge. They were flat, on a balance, approximately 5 feet by 5 feet. When Sophie was little she loved going into the warehouse with her grandfather. The smells of the different cheeses and the smoked bacon lingered long after she left the warehouse. Every visits her grandfather would weigh her on the huge scale. She looked just like a little dot in the middle. He wasn't an overly talkative man but he would talk to Sophie about his work and what he could remember of his visits to Holland as a child. When he laughed, which wasn't that often, his voice became hoarse and his eyes twinkled. Her grandmother wasn't very educated; most women in that era weren't. She had no concept of worldly affairs and her husband had whatever she wanted to be delivered. Her role was to keep the house, cook and look after the children. Hannah's mother was typical of her generation, and the one that followed. Hannah just copied what her mother did. Her background was to have very severe ramifications for her. She had high expectations of others but none of the skills to participate herself She very often found herself trusting the wrong people.

Sophie was determined not to be like her mother and her mother. Her father was adamant that education was the all-important thing and that she wasn't to work in a factory. She didn't, she was lucky and acquired office skills. This enabled her to have a good job so that she could save and buy her own house in Suffolk but, after 16 years of marriage, she became divorced and a single parent.

Within two years of Sophie's divorce, she found herself in the path of a Tsunami! The work in brokerage found her with a common ailment for those using any sort of keyboard without ergonomics being taken into account, RSI (repetitive strain injury) and she found herself off work for longer than she had ever been before. To make matters worse, she had just met someone to share her life with her and her daughter. A wonderful man, easy going, with two children of his own that he had to pay maintenance for, as he too had been divorced for two years. How could she ask anyone to take her on with all her commitments? She wanted to sell the house but, both her daughter and new partner, John, felt too many changes so soon were not in anyone's best interest. All the time she kept thinking, what if I can never work again, what if John's ex-wife asked for more maintenance, she had kept trying! What if the strain of trying to cope broke up their relationship, where would that leave her daughter, she'd already been through enough!

Sophie started to look at what work was available to her. Not an easy one. All the doctors she had seen so far had ruled out any sort of keyboard work ever again. "Even receptionists these days need to use a keyboard" she was told. Gone are the days when you just had to look good and smile and do the "meet and greet", now you were expected to be able to use a keyboard to check appointments, identify where staff were, their schedules and booking appointments, everything was done on the computer! It was no good looking at local shops and supermarkets because they too used keyboards and besides, her hands had become so weak that she couldn't possibly lift anything without dropping it! She had a keen mind and more qualifications than most but, wouldn't you know it, they were all linked to clerical/administration. Sophie had to go and seek advice from Occupational doctors to try and find something, which she would be able to do and get some sort of remuneration; all she got was the shrugging of shoulders and arm waving.

Two years had gone by now with Sophie on unemployment benefit and we all know how far that meagre money stretches! As expected, John's ex-wife kept asking for more money and kept bringing in solicitors even though she knew she couldn't get "blood out of a stone"! Things were becoming more and more difficult and Sophie really hated being on benefits. Then there was a light at the end of the tunnel. A contact had suggested Sophie had a chat with the local University to see what courses were available to help make her more employable. Also, all the help and advice and pushing Sophie in the right direction, were all under one roof why hadn't Sophie thought of this before because many years ago she had worked at the university when it was a college. Well, this proved to be Sophie's saving grace. There was a degree course which would work around Sophie's disability and, as a mature student, she could get a grant as she didn't get any maintenance from her ex-husband, she could get extra for her daughter and, if necessary, get a loan that only had to be paid off when she was in employment and earning over a certain limit. Her prayers had been answered!

It wasn't easy running a home and studying, most times into the early hours. As Sophie couldn't write too well because of her hands and using a computer wasn't easy either, whatever she did had to be planned out well so that she could get plenty of breaks in between using her hands so that her condition didn't mean she was "pill-popping" all the time. There's only so much Tramadol one can take before it muddles the brain!

Sophie got through the first year and only had another 15 months to go. The beauty of studying when you're mature is that if you already have qualifications you can use them to harness a shorter course. All was going well, perhaps a bit too well. At the end of the first week back at uni, Sophie had an accident. The chair she was sitting on evidently had metal fatigue and the back legs collapsed somersaulting Sophie backwards into the table behind where she hit her head and was then thrown under said table and hit her head on the floor rendering her unconscious. There was a laceration at the base of the skull and headaches for eight months. The main problem was that Sophie was left with retrograde amnesia. She couldn't remember what she was supposed to be doing at certain times of the day or what lecture theatre she was supposed to be in. Also, she was experiencing problems with her right eye. Doctors couldn't identify what was wrong but, thankfully, her optician did. As Sophie had only had an X-ray and not a brain scan doctors hadn't realised that her brain had a contusion, which left her with only partial peripheral vision in her right eye. She needed to drive to uni, how was she to maintain her own mobility and independence if she couldn't drive? Thankfully, after weeks of checks, the vision didn't deteriorate any more and Sophie was allowed to drive. It was a very dark time for Sophie, her daughter, and John. The head injury had caused outbursts, depression, pain and desperation that Sophie's dreams were all going to be flushed down the drain!

As Sophie's head injury became less and less of a trauma everything began to settle down and life eventually got back to normal. One good thing, which came out of the injury, was that Sophie's memory took on a more dramatic turn. She was able to visualise more and more of what she had seen and read and this helped her get her degree and she eventually started back to work. What is it they say, times can be black just before dawn? The dawn definitely began to shine for Sophie and they all began to have better times. Life was beginning to look good again.

Chapter 2

Life was being very good to them and then the inevitable happened, Randall's cancer had come back but, now, in a different place. A cell had escaped and had been playing hide and seek! More and more tests followed and courses of treatment but this time it wouldn't go away it was just kept in control. Randall and Hannah felt as if they had been kicked in the teeth!

What was the plan of action now? Obviously, the family had to be told, especially Sophie, the eldest, who lived close by and would be the one to look after them, come what may! It had always been Sophie and John who took both Randall and Hannah to their hospital appointments. The doctor's surgery being just up the road meant that for quite a long while Randall and Hannah could get to the doctor's on their own. Now Sophie and John would have to go to all appointments to make sure that both of them were completely understanding exactly what they were being told. Randall would sometimes only tell people what he wanted them to hear. Now was not the time to sweep everything under the carpet and pretend that nothing was happening.

The cancer was kept in check with hormone tablets. Most of the time they worked well with just a little adjustment.

Randall did find that these tablets not only developed his chest but also gave him mood swings. There were times when he would become very weepy. Sophie joked that now he knew just what it was like to be a woman! Sophie also noticed that he slept a lot more and began to retain water. His legs would swell up and sometimes the skin would break; also his walking was becoming more of a sway, even with his walking stick.

One day Randall got a letter from the hospital. He insisted it had told him that cancer in his spine had gone away. Sophie read the letter and had to explain that cancer hadn't "gone away" but was just being kept in check. The look on Randall's face told her that she hadn't told him what he wanted to hear. A hospital appointment was due within a week and so they <u>all</u> went up to the hospital. Again, Randall told the consultant just how marvellous it was that cancer in his spine had "gone away"! The consultant looked at them all one by one. Sophie knew what was coming. No, he said, it hadn't gone away, it was just being kept in check. It would have to be monitored to make sure it could be kept in check. The journey home was only a couple of miles but it seemed like an eternity. After a while Randall seemed to settle his life down to one of just taking the tablets, having all his checks and trying to keep positive.

John and Sophie were just beginning to get back onto an even keel. Now a big decision had to be made. Sophie reduced her hours at work and made herself more readily available to take Randall for his cancer checks at the hospital. More and more his balance went and more and more his demeanour became subdued. More and more outings up and down the coast were called for to keep serenity! Then one fatal day one false step ended life, as they had all known it. Randall had tried to open the garage door and fell backwards hitting his head on the concrete. Hannah, usually the one dependent on Randall, couldn't lift him or ring for help because of her deafness so she had to seek help from the one and only neighbour who happened to be at home at the time. What a God send she was, she rang for an ambulance so that Randall could be taken to hospital and then took Hannah indoors for a sweet tea to help with the shock. She then phoned Sophie. Of all the days for Sophie to be over 20 miles away at physiotherapy it had to be today! Sophie wasn't driving because of a hand injury. How on earth was she to get home, John was out on the road and unable to be reached. Sophie's long-term friend was on a two-day break and was able to come to her rescue! By the time she reached Hannah the neighbour had managed to "wash most of the blood away" but from the amount of blood that was left it was apparent that this injury that Randall had sustained was bad, very bad.

Thank goodness for a good neighbour who looked after Hannah whilst waiting for the ambulance and Sophie. Once Sophie knew that her mother was calm and composed and John could look after Hannah Sophie was able to get to the hospital to check on her father. Randall had sustained such a severe head injury that he had a bleed on the brain. He was unconscious nearly all the time and all that anyone could do was wait and see whether he would recover or the injury would take his life. This was very possible because now Randall was 87 years old!

The doctors were very concerned for Randall, there had been a severe bleed to the brain and it had been worse due to the Warfarin he was taking because of his heart. The blood was so thin now that he just bled and bled internally. Sophie knew it would take time for Randall to be in a more positive position, if at all. She quickly telephoned her brother to let him know that their father was in a very bad way and that she wasn't sure he would pull through. What a surprise she got when her sister- in-law rebuffed her! "Don't you phone him he's got enough on his plate" she was told? Sophie couldn't believe the attitude. Sophie did what most people would do and decided to be there for her parents come what may. What Sophie didn't know was that her brother's business was in trouble yet again! It was some months before she was able to find out what was going on.

Sophie and her father had always been very close, with similar temperaments, as her mother kept telling her. When Sophie was first married and moved into her own home she had a premonition that her father had an accident in his car on the ice. She telephoned home to her mother who had said that Randall had decided to walk to work because of the ice. A couple of hours later Sophie received a call telling her that her father had, at the last minute, decided to take his car and had crashed into a lorry. Thankfully he was only shaken up but, just like once before, he and Sophie had been linked psychically. Sophie just couldn't understand why, at this particular time, she had not felt this link to Randall to allow her to help him. She thought back to when she was a child and the family had taken a cottage holiday. Her mum and dad had a bedroom on one side of the cottage and she and her brother had a bedroom on the other side. Hannah had told her that during one of the nights she was awoken by Randall talking; she couldn't hear what he was saying and at first thought that he was just talking in his sleep. When she listened more closely she could hear another voice. Randall was clearly asleep but this other voice could be heard across the landing. Hannah had gotten out of bed to where the other voice was coming from. She entered the bedroom on the far side of the landing to hear and see Sophie talking. Sophie was alsoclearly asleep. Hannah still couldn't make out what was beingspoken but it was obvious to her that Randall and Sophie weredeep in conversation in their sleep. Hannah always said the pair of them were psychically linked.

The weeks in the hospital seemed endless whilst the medical team tried to get Randall well. Randall was becoming more and more depressed, even though Sophie and John took Hannah to the hospital to see Randall every day he became more and more anxious and desperate to get back home. Sophie and John used to pick up Hannah every morning and take her to see Randall and then take her shopping or for a ride out to the coast for a walk to keep her mind off how bad Randall was and hoped that she would sleep of a night to be ready in case Randall took a turn for the worse.

Randall was told that he couldn't drive for three months at least until his brain had settled down. He never got to drive again as his car was taken away from him.

During this time Sophie had made regular emails to her brother because, evidently, he was out on the road and couldn't be contacted by a call but arrangements were made for him to collect Sophie at their parent's house so that they could all go together. On one occasion he did say he would pick her up en-route but this never happened and she had to make her own way to the hospital. Looking back her brother didn't seem pleased to see her and brushed the whole incident of not picking her up as a misunderstanding. She later came to believe it was a ploy to keep her out of the picture!

It was necessary that physiotherapists and occupational therapists visit the bungalow to make sure that the help that was going to be put in place for Randall was appropriate for his needs mainly, and to assist Hannah; with walking frames, bed rests, regular visits and updates on progress. It was important to get back Randall's confidence and enable him to eventually be independent again. Unfortunately, this never had a chance to work because of the intervention of others… "isolate and control"!

It was all arranged that a small ambulance would get Randall home. When the day came there wasn't an ambulance available. Typical! Frantic telephone calls were made and eventually, the hospital organised a Charity to make arrangements for Randall's homecoming. They managed to get him up the path to the front door and then disaster struck again in his haste, Randall kicked the front doorstep and flung himself into the hallway. John and Sophie both lunged forward to get Randall to his feet and into a chair. After removing his coat and getting him a cup of tea Randall settled down but he did look very pale. He spent a lot of time sleeping and every day John and Sophie spent time with Randall and Hannah. Carers were organised by the hospital to help with personal care and walking but, before long, Randall insisted he didn't want them. It took a lot of persuasions to keep a care plan in place; not only to help Randall but also to helpHannah. They were both getting older now and looking very strained with all the events that had occurred over the months.Sophie and John tried hard to get things back to some sort of "normal". They never would be normal ever again!

Randall came home on his sister's birthday! Physios went

in and put all the necessary equipment in place to help. The biggest problem was Randall's lack of confidence and his unwillingness to walk. He was so frightened of falling that it was easier for him to just sit in a chair so Sophie and John went around daily to make sure all was well and that Randall and Hannah were okay with carers that the hospital had put in for support and medication. Food and cleaning were undertaken by Sophie and John. It became more and more troubling when Randall kept insisting that the carers should get him his Warfarin. He was not allowed his Warfarin for three months and had been put on coagulants so that the brain bleed could be dealt with. The doctor had to be informed of this so that the carers didn't inadvertently give him both coagulants and anti- coagulants, which would have had a more adverse effect on his mental stability. This problem of mental stability became more and more of an issue. Randall was becoming irritable with carers, Hannah, Sophie and John and other family members. His sister was concerned for him.

One Saturday Sophie went around to see her parents and do her usual housework for them and was surprised to see her brother. He normally only turned up once or twice a month but now had started turning up once a week. Good thought Sophie, it's taken a catastrophe to make him realise that his parents are getting older and need to see BOTH their children and get support. Wrong! Whilst Hannah was in the kitchen and out of earshot Sophie's brother started his onslaught. He was telling Randall that he was going to take him out here and there and everything was going to be fine and absolutely fantastic! Sophie, being her usual practical self, said that as the ambulance crew had difficulty getting Randall out of the house and up and down the pathway to the ambulance that the first thing to get done was a ramp made and a wider path!

With that Sophie's brother told her to "keep her fat f... mouth shut", and raised his hand as if to hit her! When Sophie, politely, told him that his manner was not only abusive but not being kind to his father she was told in no uncertain terms to leave the residence and not come back! Sophie could see that her father was very distressed by witnessing this attempt at physical assault. Whether he understood what was being said she never knew but, being a dutiful daughter, she left the premises reminding her younger brother that he wasn't the owner of their parents' home and it was up to them to tell her to leave not him! In months to come Sophie would realise that she had never said a truer word but that it was already too late! If only we could be a fly on the wall and hear what others truly had in their minds and hearts. In months to come it became obvious to all members of the family that a plan had been hatched to sell the bungalow and put Randall and Hannah in a flat.

Sophie never knew whether her brother fell short of actually hitting her because the police were already involved with her brother's family or her "expertise" in boxing! Randall taught her how to box so that she could defend herself if necessary; and, as her brother was not that good at boxing Sophie always had to fight his battles for him. Sophie made contact with her parents' neighbour and told her of the abuse that had just taken place and asked her to ring her if anything happened which she felt uneasy about. This neighbour had at times found it difficult for her knock to be answered and had phoned in the past to raise an alarm. Before long the HEARS alarms that were put in place were dispensed with and the carers were told to leave. Why? Also, prior to the fall, Randall had said that Sophie's brother was taking over doing the hospital visits with him and that Sophie didn't need to bother with this anymore. Why? He had never done that **ever** before and been more than keen that Sophie undertook all the care and attention. Why? Randall's garden with flowers and vegetables had been his life, his way of relaxing, but these were beginning to be reduced in size and turned over to shingles instead of lawns.

Chapter 3

John and Sophie very quickly realised that more was going to be needed to give respite for both Randall and Hannah. An architect was required to draw up plans to see how John and Sophie's house could be extended and made more purpose built to allow them to help in a more practical way without taking away any independence from Randall and Hannah but still allowing for overseeing to make sure all health and safety issues were covered. With Randall's cancer and now this head injury it was possible that Hannah would need a break away from him from time to time for respite, especially as she had a heart problem and which Sophie used to take her to the hospital for checks. Or, it might even be that Randall would want a different set of four walls to look at and French doors onto the garden to allow easy access for better days and times. Within two and a half months the plans were approved so that work could start in the Spring. The plans extended theback of the house so that it linked up with the detached garage.It was the garage which was converted into a bedroom witha wet room, ideal for immobility use. The internal doorallowed easy access to the extended kitchen diner so thatRandall and Hannah could make their own teas, breakfasts, orwhatever they wanted so that they could keep their own independence. Sophie procured a rather large "Ship's Bell" which Randall could easily ring. It was loud enough to be heard all over the house to summon for help!

All was going well until Sophie fell out onto the patio! Half her body was outdoors and the feet and ankles were inside. Her body was twisted and her back felt as if it was broken, as she couldn't lift herself. More hospital intervention but, now, it was for her. No broken bones the doctor said but, she said "you might just as well have broken them because it will be at least six weeks before you will start to be able to put your own shoes on and walk without crutches"! It was actually seven weeks before she could give John his slippers back as they were the only things that would fit on her swollen feet! John had to get and do whatever Randall and Hannah needed on his own during this time.

When next Sophie saw her parents there had been a change in their demeanour and in Randall, there was a distinct hostility. At this time it was all believed to be part of the head injury but in months to come, it became increasingly clear that more was going on behind the scenes than was apparent. As Sophie was later to find out a family member had been making various visits to Randall and Hannah and getting them to sign Third Party paperwork to allow access to their accounts, their savings, and their pensions and also to allow the sale of their home and their possessions which they had accrued through all the years of their marriage; over 68 years!

In the months and years that followed Sophie investigated. She checked her diaries and her emails and texts. Bit by bit she pieced together the undercurrents that should have alerted her that something wasn't right. Sideways glances from other family members had meant that others must have had an idea of what was going on but nothing wassaid. Surely if you know that someone is being or about to beused and abused you would point out to other family members that you had a suspicion. Sophie remembered other such instances relating to other family members and still, it didn't resonate with her. Sophie would never have behaved in this way and this is probably why she didn't even suspect any wrongdoing. If Sophie had thought something was not quite right she would have made contact with others to find out whether suspicions were true or not. Evidently, not all peoplethink the same way as Sophie!

Normally her Extra Sensory Perception gave her knowledge of problems and inconsistencies but, this time, she never picked up on her gut instincts. Who would suspect that a family member with the same blood running through their veins would do such a thing to their supposedly loved ones? It had often been reported in the newspapers about family theft, Sophie would never have thought that a member of her family would stoop so low and most definitely not in the manner in which it would be brought about!

The last gathering with some of Randall's family, especially his sister, was an August Bar-B-Que just before Randall's terrible fall. On that day Randall looked like he hadn't had a restive sleep for days and Hannah sat away from Randall's side of the family. Sophie thought at the time that her parents had had a difference of opinion or that Hannah wanted her traditional roast indoors and not "finger" food in the garden with "all those flies"! Neither of her parents interacted with the others on that day, perhaps with a nod or a few words but, on reflection, they weren't their usual chatty selves. The photos that had been taken of a trip to the coast only a short while before shows them both bright, happy, smart and obviously enjoying themselves. Were things in the pipeline even then? Later when Sophie checked the dates she found that they coincided with meetings with Creditors and Liquidators for her brother's business. The final meeting was just weeks before the move from their home to that dismal little flat! The saying is right, you can choose your friends but you can't choose your family! It wasn't many weeks after this Bar-B-Que that Randall had that dreadful fall. Something so simple as going to the garage changed all their lives forever. An overbalance, a fall on concrete, the thud to the head, the blood, so much blood, and then unconsciousness.

The building of the basic extension to help Randall and Hannah took some 12 weeks but then add to that all the days and weeks in between of concrete drying and plastering drying, waiting on heating engineers and the electricians and glaziers and flooring made it six months plus as then there was appropriate appliances and decorating and that took some more time. For all this time Sophie and John were living on a building site, well it felt as if they were! For Sophie with her problems and John trying to negate the workmen to keep to their time schedules the pair of them were feeling quite low both financially, healthily and mentally. When they were later to realise that all their efforts to help and support Randall and Hannah had been in vain it was a bitter pill to swallow! However, they continued with the plan. One of Sophie's cousins had asked her why she was making her house bigger when most people, as they get older, decide to downsize. Sophie was tempted to explain to him what had happened and why it was necessary but then she may well have found that Randall and Hannah would have been told and their response would have been "no, you save your money"! Sophie knew her duty and knew what had to be done!

Chapter 4

Christmas was approaching and food was needed for Randall and Hannah as they always had Sophie's brother and family up for Christmas Eve. Although Sophie had made sure she wasn't around on the day that her brother was up she had gotten extra food in for that and had even asked her mum and dad if they wanted her to cook it for them. That way they only had to dish it all up. They declined this offer saying that as Sophie's brother was coming up earlier in the day he would be able to arrange all that for them. Sophie wasn't convinced but she didn't want to interfere with their plans. She gave them their card and pressies and just enquired when they thought she could pop around again over Christmas. To this Randall said that Sophie's brother and family would be up from Christmas Eve until Boxing day late afternoon. Sophie and John and their immediate family wished them well for Christmas and left, ready to put their own arrangements in place.

It was a strange Christmas that year and, as it turned out, for a couple of Christmas to come. Previously when Sophie's brother and family came on Christmas Eve it left Christmas Day for Randall and Hannah and Sophie's daughter and family to come to hers and then on Boxing Day Sophie's daughter would return the meal. It had worked that way for years since Sophie's brother entertained others on Christmas Day and Boxing Day.

After Boxing Day when Sophie visited her parents she was met with hostility from her father when she asked him if they had had a nice time. It turned out that her brother had NOT turned up for the whole of Christmas as they had expected but just his usual Christmas Eve. When asked why they hadn't phoned her so that Sophie and her family could have gone to Randall and Hannah's and organised all the catering for them she was met with absurdities from Randall and a lot of eyebrow-raising from Hannah. To cap it all Randall then went into a tirade about not receiving a Christmas card from Sophie and John and that she hadn't given them any presents. When Sophie showed her father that her Christmas card was on the window sill with all the other cards and that the book she had gotten him for his present was sitting on the table and her mother's perfume, which she got for her every year, was on the dressing table in the bedroom! Randall was adamant! No, she hadn't given them the cards and presents before Christmas, she had put them through the post. When asked how his very large book had managed to be put through a very tiny letterbox Randall couldn't explain. No mention of the pots and Spring bulbs that she had planted for him to try and lift his spirits.

You can imagine how hurt and upset this made Sophie. More and more Randall was losing his grasp on events as they took place. More and more there came this pressing need for trying to get the builders to move forward with the extensions. More and more Sophie and John were put under considerable strain and expense to try and complete a 12-month plan, organise, and build it into six months! It was during this start of excavations that Sophie fell out of the French doors onto the patio and then the ten weeks of inaction and pain!

By the time that May came, Sophie was able to move about a lot more. She had received a text from Randall saying thank you for her mother's birthday card but not a word about the birthday card she had given Randall or the extra pots and bulbs. He had become very distant and most of the time it was only Hannah who greeted them and thanked them for getting shopping and helping her. For some reason when Randall had told Sophie that her brother was getting all their food and not to bother to get anything for them anymore it was, in fact, Randall that was getting food online. Sophie's brother had shown their 87-year-old father how to shop online so that it could be delivered and so he could make fewer visits to his parents! Hannah had kept phoning Sophie to say that the "man with the van" hadn't brought their shopping so could she pick up a few items? Naturally Sophie said yes and had, at first, thought that the shopping list that they made out for her brother had been incomplete. It was over a month before she got the truth out of them. At the time Sophie couldn't understand this entire "cloak and dagger" attitude and thought it was because of the altercation that had taken place between her and her brother before Christmas. It later transpired that lies had been told to her parents and they were bound to secrecy: a bit difficult when one of them has had such a bad head injury that he couldn't think straight and the other was told not to divulge what was going on and in the end was found not to really know what was going on at all.

Within a few months Sophie's daughter and her children arrived at hers in floods of tears and said that they would never see Randall and Hannah again alive! Randall had told her that he was moving away into a flat. Hannah said that the flat had a bus stop right outside so that she could go shopping. This was very, very strange. Hannah had not been on a bus in years and certainly wouldn't go out on her own. She never even hung the washing out on her own now. What about Randall's cancer checks? Sophie had to spend the whole of the rest of the day consoling her daughter and grandchildren. Her grandchildren were so upset to see their mother in tears. Randall had told his granddaughter that she wasn't to tell Sophie about them moving. Sophie's daughter politely told her grandfather that she and her mother never ever keptsecrets from each other and she wasn't about to start now. Evidently, Randall was marching around with his hands in theair going from room to room as if he was having a psychotic attack!

Sophie went around to see Randall and Hannah find out what on earth was going on. Randall went into floods of tears and Sophie had to put her arms around him and ask him what on earth was going on and why was he so very upset. It became apparent that Sophie's brother was at the bottom of it all. His wife had arranged a flat for them to view to move into. Randall wasn't happy about this flat, it was small and he didn't know anybody, he then went on to say that all his medical notes were being sent to a general practitioner near Sophie's brother ready for their move. Sophie asked them both did they want to move out of their bungalow. Hannah didn't say a word but Randall went into floods of tears again and said he had been told that he couldn't keep messing his daughter-in-law about and he must go as she had arranged everything for them. Sophie reminded him that he didn't have to go anywhere if he didn't want to and that he was the master of his own decisions. That if they wanted to move out of their bungalow and away from her and her family that was fine but, more importantly, they had never expressed this wish before and had been quite adamant that they were going to die in their own bed in their bungalow and be taken from their bungalow by funeral directors when they died! However, if they were having problems coping and didn't want Sophie to keep going around helping them that was fine but, and this was a big but, they had to be sure it was what they wanted and not what somebody else was telling them. Everything eventually calmed down and before she left Randall had said he would have a word with his son to say that he wasn't going to move after all.

On further visits Sophie didn't hear any more about the move or that there had been any altercation between Randall and his son and daughter-in-law. However, some weeks went by and then Sophie got a telephone call from Randall asking her to come around and look after her mother. Naturally, she said yes! Randall kept on apologising for asking her to help. Said that he couldn't reach her brother, his wife or his children.

Strange, Sophie had always been there to help. What was going on? Randall said that his blood levels for his Warfarin were not good and that the doctor had called an ambulance for him to go to the hospital. Sophie turned up just as they were loading Randall onto the ambulance. She told her father not to worry, she would get to the hospital later to check on him, and that she would check on Hannah and make sure she was okay.

When John and Sophie arrived Hannah was sitting on a chair surrounded by boxes. John took one look and said he had to go outside because he felt angry! Sophie explained to Hannah that she would stay with her for a while and then check on Randall at the hospital. Hannah just kept looking at the floor, barely raising her eyes at Sophie. In the end, Sophie had to ask her if she was moving. Hannah said yes, that Sophie's brother had arranged it all. When asked where they were moving to she said she didn't know, she had no address and promised that they would phone Sophie with the address and phone number before they moved which, she thought, would be at the end of May. By the end of May, this had not happened. The move happened at the end of June and there had been no phone call, or mention of a date when Sophie and John called to check on both Randall and Hannah over the coming weeks. There wasn't anything said that led them to believe that Randall and Hannah were moving away for good at all.

On Monday, which turned out to be the day after the weekend move, Sophie and John went around to see Randall and Hannah and found they had moved with their bed, television, armchairs, and the boxes that had adorned the lounge. Everything else seemed to be in place. The Hoover was still there which had been bought just before Randall's fall, together with the new fridge-freezer, and the wardrobes still had contents in them and the dining furniture was still there. Nothing to suggest that they weren't coming back. Sophie and John just waited and checked to see if Randall and Hannah would telephone or return to their beloved home. This never happened ever again. Their home was put up for sale and Randall and Hannah had, it turned out, been made to sign *Third Party* documentation allowing Sophie's brother total control over their bank accounts, savings, and the sale of their property. This had been done without any family knowledge, their Solicitor of over 26 years had no knowledge of their move and was still in receipt of their Wills. He had no idea about the sale of their property. There was no Power of Attorney in place!

After Randall's death, Sophie checked to see if a Will and Probate had been lodged. There had been, after all, some £230,000 from the sale of the property and accounts but, as she suspected, all monies had been extracted via Third Party with no reference made to the usual Government Offices or Inland Revenue for the tax which should have been paid as this was unearned income!

Chapter 5

A few weeks went by and still no news. Sophie went around to see her mother and father's neighbours. They too were dismayed as they had tried to make contact and didn't know what was going on. No mention was ever made to them that a move was imminent. Even the window cleaner didn't know they were moving and he chatted to them all the time and would re-iterate conversations back to Sophie.

Sophie got a telephone call from her dad's only remaining sibling. She said that she had found out where her mother and father were and that she felt compelled to tell her where they were and that she had only just found out herself. She had been phoning every Sunday, as always, with no response and then found that they had been moved into a flat. She had found out that as soon as Randall had gone into this flat his health had changed for the worse and that he had spent weeks in the hospital nearest to where they were now living. Arrangements were made to pick this aunt up and they all go to visit Randall and Hannah. At the last minute, this visit was postponed due to hospital appointments but, by the time the next visit was to be arranged, Randall's sister had got her eldest daughter and son-in-law to take her to the hospital and then to visit Hannah.

It was nearly nine o'clock one night when Sophie got a

call from this aunt and cousin and her husband. It was difficult to make out exactly what was being said as they all wanted to talk at the same time. In the background, Sophie's aunt was distraught saying that she went to the hospital but that her "brother wasn't there" and she needed to "know where my brother is"! It then transpired that this party had then gone onto where Randall and Hannah were living and that it was found that the flat was not appropriate to their needs or Hannah being looked after properly. They said that necessary items of shopping had been put up on top shelving where Hannah couldn't possibly reach. She couldn't reach the box of tea bags so hadn't had tea; the television was not wired up so that she could see the television. All that needed to be done immediately was sorted for Hannah but still had no idea of where Randall was. Hannah said he'd been taken to hospital but she didn't know which one (if they had been in their own home she would have known which hospital) and that in the weeks that he had been in hospital she had only been taken by her son once to see her husband!

All this had fuelled all the disquiet that Sophie had had to listen to from the three family members who had, unknowingly to Sophie, taken this immediate action.

Sophie didn't know exactly where her parents were except for the address her aunt had given her only days before and she told her that she only had one course of action open to her; to call the police and say her father was a missing person! This she did through her own area police who contacted the police in that area. After a time the police contacted Sophie and her aunt and said that they had made contact with Sophie's brother where others just got a phone that kept ringing and that they told him that he had to let family members know what was going on! They found out that Randall was thought to have been discharged back home but hadn't and been placed in another ward and the computer hadn't picked this up! They said he was fine. Turned out he wasn't, and that Hannah was fine which, unfortunately, also wasn't true! To cut a long story short Randall's health had changed so badly because of the move that he became the recipient of a Safeguarding Order being put in place by the paramedic in charge!

Sophie and her aunt (from their own phones) phoned Sophie's brother but got no reply (so much for police intervention and compliance)! Sophie decided to leave a message on the answering machine. Very late that night, after the police had called, Sophie got a telephone call from her sister-in-law. Sophie said very little as, typically, her sister-in-law, as usual, was in a blustering mood and abusive and most of the words just ran into one. Almost incomprehensible! The duration of this call was some two hours long! Granted much of this abuse was directed at Randall and Hannah. Sophie listened, took notes and eventually told her sister-in-law that she was recording the call. This had the desired effect of calming her down a little. To break this call down into basics, it was said that Randall and Hannah were being a nuisance.

Randall was "wetting and defecating bedding andclothes" and she "wasn't prepared to wash dirty linen"! Also,"he's lazy and won't get out of the chair"! Sophie felt like crying; to have her parents spoken about so unsympathetically was very trying for her. Sophie wanted to ask why, if they were such nuisances, were they were removed from their home where they had all the support and medical care they needed.

Sophie knew from the work she had done in the past that if you can keep cool and listen eventually the other party give over all the information and facts you need. She soon learned why. Her sister-in-law went on to say how, when asked, Randall had told her that he would not give her the £5,000 she needed to pay her mortgage. She went to great lengths to say how he "didn't care that his grandsons might end up without a roof over their heads" and how her father would have willingly given them a cheque for the mortgage. She went on to say that Sophie's brother had told her that she shouldn't have asked for money. Sophie thought on this; interesting, had he already asked for the money and now Randall was being asked for money twice? What Sophie was finding difficult was the fact that her sister-in-law's father had died and left her a half-share in his house so why did she need £5,000?

At this point, Sophie decided to offer a sympathetic ear in the hope that her sister-in- law would divulge more information. Already Sophie was beginning to realise that the abuse and attempt of assault on her and the clandestine removal of Randall and Hannah from their home were to keep Sophie and the rest of the family at a distance to allow lies, and deceit to induce coercion of signatures to paperwork to allow access to their money. Her sister-in-law went on to say that Randall liked to "divide and rule"! Funny that that's what someone else had said about Sophie's brother and his wife! Also, lots of past memories of conversations kept flooding back. The time that she had said that the property's windows needed replacing for security and keeping the place warm and that Randall, after a conversation with his son, had said that he'd been told that new windows weren't necessary and to save the money. What did the money need to be saved for? Actually, Sophie's suggestion was right as the property was broken into and items stolen within the year!

Sophie decided that now she had to get someone else involved to keep an ear and eye on what was going on, whilst she was getting hospital treatment. The phone calls received were very informative. Both Randall and Hannah, it was said, had been a "nuisance" to those looking after them. "This had been said before"! "They", Randall and Hannah, "were expecting too much", and "we have to work and don't have the time to keep running around"! These same remarks kept cropping up time and time again. How can one's own parents be a nuisance? They couldn't help getting older and having complex needs. Nobody plans to become dependent on others, it just creeps up on one. Bit by bit easy tasks become difficult and as soon as one's health takes a dramatic turn it is natural to seek the help and support of those who are "supposed" to love you! All the feedback that Sophie got began to show a picture and not a very nice one at that. Lots of suspicions but that alone would not be enough to show others what was going on. Hard facts and evidence would be needed.

Sophie, John and one other person went down to see Randall in the hospital to make sure that he was receiving the care that he needed and then on to see Hannah to let her know where Randall was, how he was and see what help she was getting and needing.

It was a 40–45 minute journey and, unfortunately, the roads were particularly bad this day. Eventually, they arrived at the hospital and then had to try and find out exactly where Randall was. The hospital was new, big and airy but, typically, when it was urgent to get to see Randall, again the technical system seemed to be unforthcoming at first. With lots of ringing around from the desk operator, Randall was found. The three of them found the ward and a doctor came to see them full of apologies. It appeared that Randall had been taken into hospital and was then returned home to the flat and then rushed back into the hospital again and put in an isolation ward with other patients who had all been infected whilst at the hospital! They were all now on the "mend" but to go in and see Randall they all had to be using protective wear, both for them and the patients. When questioning the doctor about this "incontinence and defecation" problem it turned out that this was not a long-term condition and had only come about with this onset of the sickness and vomiting virus which had been transmitted to him, and others, whilst in hospital: hence all the apologising. Further discussions with the doctor about Randall's supposedly deteriorating condition that would need to put him in a Care Home, as told by Sophie's sister-in-law, were quite unfounded. Randall had been responding to treatment and was likely to be sent home to Hannah within a week.

Suitably suited up with personal protective wear the three of them went into the Ward. The look on Randall's face when he saw that he had visitors was a sight to behold he was clearly over the moon to see them, but he had aged greatly. He was looking rather thin, his complexion was grey and his arms were full of bruises. He had none of the usual personal things that people have around them in the hospital like his slippers, his glasses to see, his toilet bag with essentials or any form of clothing like a cardigan for sitting in a chair when out of bed. He had no money either and Sophie had to leave him £5 so that he could phone his wife!

Sophie hugged her dad and his face lit up! He thanked her for coming "all that way"? He and Hannah had been told that Sophie and John were moving to Leicester (the ploy used to get them to move from their home). "No, Dad," Sophie said, "it was you and Mum that moved; we are still living where we have lived for the last 18 odd years!" Randall seemed to have trouble getting his head around that one. Sophie went on, "Why would I move to Leicester when my daughter and grandchildren are all living just up the road from me?" She could see him trying to make sense of it and then the look of realisation that he and Hannah had been duped. That look would haunt Sophie. Randall took both of Sophie's hands in his and said, "I need you to do something for me "ducks", I need you to find out for me where all my money has gone!" Sophie, John and their witness looked at each other. They looked around at the other patients and could see one or two of them nodding as if they too knew what was happening. The patient in the corner, opposite Randall's bed, put a thumbs up and smiled. Randall went on, "There's a Trust Fund set up for £30,000, my pension, the ISA's and the Building Society Account." Sophie agreed to investigate as far as she could. She asked if a Power of Attorney had been set up because she said that it would be difficult to over turn a Power of Attorney without good cause. Randall replied, "No, not a Power of Attorney but I did sign something." Sophie pushed him further as to what he had signed and he said that he didn't know. That was not her father, he would never have signed anything without knowing what it was. Alarm bells began to ring. Still holding Sophie's hands and gripping them Randall told Sophie to promise to look after her mother, to which she agreed. It was hard to see and hear the words of a broken man. Sophie asked Randall if Hannah had been in to see him.

He replied, "Only once when I first came into the hospital." This she verified with Hannah and it related to the very first hospitalisation soon after they were removed from their hometo the flat that her brother and sister-in-law had set up. That was some four months earlier! Sophie didn't want to dwell onwhat she had been told and started talking about how everyone was doing to lighten the mood. At this point, a male nurse came into the Ward and tried to push Randall into having some toast. He asked questions about Randall's visitors and said he knew who they were because Randall kept talking about his son-in-law and his car, and when questioned, confirmed that they had been the only visitors in all the time that Randall was there, whilst he was on duty! On theirleaving the Ward, Randall asked for a mobile phone so that he could phone Hannah. Sophie said yes she would get him one. What had happened to the one he had?

The three of them said their goodbyes, saying that they were going to see Hannah and make sure that she was okay. Although smiling back at Randall, when out of eyesight they were all very gloomy going over what Randall had said, what the doctor and nurse said and the looks on the faces of the patients. They chatted all the way to Hannah's about what was suspected of going on.

When they got to Hannah's she equally was very pleased to see them. Briefly, she was told of how Randall was and that within a week he should be home. Hannah was so pleased to see her niece and asked lots of questions about the family. She gave a tour of her little flat and it became apparent that the flat was totally inadequate for Randall and Hannah's needs; it was only a quarter of the size of their bungalow!

Hannah wasn't wearing her hearing aid and said she couldn't find it. She said she had trouble hearing if they all talked at once. Sophie had known this for years and had always very carefully mouthed her words so that Hannah could lip-read. They tried to find her hearing aid but couldn't. Whilst looking they noticed that only one set of bedding was in the flat and this was on the bed. Hannah had always had plenty of everything. Her motto was "one on, one in the wash and one spare"! None of her best clothes was hanging in the wardrobe or in the drawers. In fact, all the clothes found were two sizes too big and were what she used for cleaning the house. None of her best clothes was there! Nobody passed comment whilst in the flat but, on their return to the car, were eagerly exchanging views and comments on what had been said and what had been seen and, more importantly, what wasn't at the flat that should have been. Everything Randall's sister and her daughter and son-in-law had said were true! It wasn't going to be an easy task but somehow something had to be done.

On Sophie's return home, she set about getting a mobile phone and began to look at what she needed to do to sort out this terrible mess that had come about purely in the name of greed. She found it totally incomprehensible that such a thing could be done to her parents. She remembered that some six years previous a conversation had been started up by her brother about releasing equity in the bungalow. Sophie had pointed out then that it was a ridiculous idea. Randall and Hannah were on Guaranteed Pension Credit, why on earth would they need more money at that time? The time to release equity is when all your savings had gone and you couldn't get help or support in one's final years! When Sophie had questioned Randall about the conversation he had said that there was no way he would ever give up the bungalow and that he and Hannah were to die there and be in their own bed! Hannah was later to say that she had no idea what was going on and always thought the move was temporary and that her bungalow was still there for her. The look on her face when she was shown the paperwork said that the property had been sold and more than two-thirds of the money was gone. She kept asking, "Am I destitute?" "Not whilst I am alive, Mum," Sophie had said. "I will look after you to the best of my ability and make sure you have all that you need but, I am sorry to say, there is not enough money to buy back your home!"

Within 48 hours of returning home, Sophie had been feeling really unwell. She spent most of the night keep getting up to go to the toilet and lying on the floor where it was cool and safe. Every time she stood up she became bent over in pain and had no choice but to sit on the toilet. Before long both the toilet and the hand basin became part of Sophie. How fortuitous that the hand basin was only inches to the left of the toilet so that both receptacles could be used at the same time. If the question had arisen as to whether to go on with life or die at this time it was more than probable that she would have said die! Yes, she had caught the same virus that Randall had! An ambulance was called but they wouldn't take Sophie to the hospital when they found out where the virus had come from as they couldn't risk having the hospital put under quarantine. John had to pick up the prescription that was left for Sophie and administer it regularly. It was nearly a week before Sophie was conscious and able to leave her bed. As soon as she was able she phoned Hannah and explained what had happened. She had been expecting Randall to return home from the hospital but he was still in the isolation ward. It was another three days before he was allowed home. Thankfully carers were put in place to take care of him and, when Sophie called, it was one of the carers who answered the phone. "Yes, both Randall and Hannah are okay. Would you like to speak to Randall?" Sophie was so pleased that her dad had gone home to be with her mother. Randall picked up the phone and began saying how pleased he had been to see them all in the hospital, thanking them for their support and saying not to worry about him. Bless him! Sophie explained what had happened and that she had the mobile that he wanted but that she couldn't get it to him until she was assured that she couldn't give him the virus back. She said she would be down to see them soon when she was "lergy free"! By the time that came around Randall was back in the hospital again. A hospital member phoned to say that he had gone back in and was "rather poorly"! What on earth had happened now?

During that night and the next morning, Sophie had tried to ring Hannah but, without success. *I bet she isn't wearing her hearing aid,* thought Sophie. She decided to ring the hospital to find out what ward Randall was on and to see if any of the staff could give her any information. She was in luck, she was put straight through to the ward and a member of staff took the phone to Randall so that she could speak to him. "Sophie" Randall kept calling out, "Yes, Dad," she said and started asking how he was. He kept saying, "Sophie, how are you," and Sophie started to talk to him again. After a while, Sophie became concerned because he didn't seem that responsive. She asked the member of staff if he was drugged.

No! came back the reply, and then she told Randall to put

thephone to the other ear if he couldn't hear properly. The staff member then said that Randall had "dropped off to sleep"! Sophie said she would call again later to find out how he was. Within hours Sophie received a call from the hospital that Randall had passed away. They said that they had phoned herbrother, as he lived closer but, (not surprisingly to Sophie), hewouldn't be attending the hospital to see his father! As it wasnow very late Sophie said that she would attend the hospital tomorrow and asked for directions to the correct people to help her see Randall in the mortuary. She tried to ring Hannahbut the phone just kept ringing and going to answer machine.There was no phone call from her brother to break the news to her. Again, no surprise! As far as Sophie was concerned he,and his family, had brought about the demise of Randall in a most despicable way. They had left him in fear for Hannah's well-being and left him with nothing tangible to live for.

Chapter 6

Sophie didn't know how to break the news to Randall's sister, she had heart problems and had to be told very gently. Her only choice was to phone the daughter who lived locally and used to see to her mother's everyday needs. As you can imagine it wasn't easy breaking this news to her cousin. It was hard for Sophie to keep her composure; she didn't want to make her cousin so sad that she couldn't handle the situation calmly with her mother! It had already been arranged for Sophie and John to go down to see her aunt and cousins before this heartbreaking news. This they continued to do.

As Sophie arrived at her cousin's she received a call, not from her brother, from his eldest son, who told her that her father was dead! She pointed out to him that it was not his responsibility to deliver the message but his father and that it should have been done straight away after the death! His reply was, "Well there's history between you and Dad." Sophie politely pointed out that that was news to her! At no time did her brother phone her himself to tell her, nor did he tell her, or any of the family, the arrangements for the funeral. Not even Randall's sister. She was heartbroken!

Sophie had to compose herself and keep calm and not betray the turmoil she was in or the anger she felt. She couldn't make matters worse for her aunt. With some soul searching it was decided that it wasn't in her aunt's best interest to see her brother at the hospital morgue. Sophie and John went on their own. When they eventually arrived staff were on a break and they had to wait for the specialist attendant to arrive.

All the staff were so helpful and understanding and Sophie felt her father was in caring hands, even though he had passed.

Randall looked so peaceful compared to the way he looked when he had been specific about what he wanted Sophie to do for him. It was as if he could clear his mind of all that had happened. She made him the promise that she would do her very best to fulfil his wishes, no matter how long it took! John and Sophie looked in on Hannah. She was really pleased to see them and it didn't seem as if she was aware of the fact that Randall had gone. Perhaps it's the shock Sophie thought. Hannah said that she still didn't know when Randall was coming home. Sophie just looked. Hadn't her brother bothered to tell her that Randall was dead? Hadn't he even bothered to get her to the hospital so that she could say her "goodbyes"? The look on Sophie's face must have said it all because Hannah held on to Sophie and said "he isn't coming home is he"! Sophie found it really hard to contain her tears and said "No, Mum, he isn't!" They both held on to each other for some time. Eventually, Sophie said, "Weren't you told?" Hannah said that Sophie's brother was looking out of the kitchen window when his son was talking to her. "Did you hear what he was saying, Mum?"

"Well no, I didn't have my hearing aid and could only catch a few words, he talks so quietly"!

Hannah asked if they wanted tea. Sophie said no but that she would make one for Hannah with plenty of sugar in it. Hannah eventually asked if Sophie was going home. "I think I had better stay with you tonight, Mum." "No," Hannah said. "If Randall has gone I had better get used to being on my own and I might as well start now!" How Sophie held in her tears she never knew but she felt physically sick with what she had been told by Hannah. She kept waiting to see if Hannah would change her mind and said that she would stay and John could go home and come back and get her or, of course, did she want to go home with them? Again, Hannah said no and that they were to go home and get some rest and that she was going to bed straight away.

John took Sophie home; by the time they got home, it was a quick cup of tea and bed. Sleep was sorely needed. They both had headaches! Surprisingly it came very quickly and without disturbance. Once the morning came Sophie felt brighter and her mind was rested for whatever lay ahead. If she had known then what more was to come she would probably have stayed in bed and never get up! Yet another phone call from her sister-in-law being abusive. "Your mother keeps asking for you, You should be here for her." Sophie politely told her, "Well, that's strange because we went to the hospital yesterday and then on to Mum's!" If her brother, sister-in-law and the children had actually been at the flat looking after Hannah, or even taken her home to their house as they should have done if they were really carers to Randall and Hannah they would have been well aware of who was with Hannah and when. The only explanation was that they were home tending to their own needs and not Hannah's in her time of need. This was a great worry to Sophie, how could she be in two places at once? As they had taken control of everything connected to Randall and Hannah, including where they lived, Sophie had to leave well alone for the moment. The hospital had told her that funeral arrangements and directors were being instructed and it would have been pretty churlish to step in and take charge at such a time. It would have been totally irreverent!

Sophie phoned the hospital for details on whether Randall's body had been released for cremation. It was necessary for delay for two doctors to confirm the death before a Certificate was released. It wasn't until Sophie got the transcripts of medical notes, nearly two years later, that she found out that Randall's death had not been expected. Was this why two doctors had to confirm death before the Certificate was issued? After nearly four days Sophie was able to get confirmation that the certificate had been issued and who was going to be the funeral director. Again, still no word from her brother about arrangements and no answer to her calls. Family members were calling to find out what the arrangements were. She could only give them the basics because that's all she knew. In their desperation for details, her cousins had phoned her brother and were met with abuse. Although not nice it did mean that they now believed Sophie when she told them all that had gone on and what she had suspected. They too had suspected something wasn't right when Randall and Hannah had left their home, which everyone knew they loved, and then didn't make contact with anyone. Sophie had her own views on this. Perhaps the telephone book with addresses and phone numbers had been taken away from them. Maybe they were told that nobody cared about them, maybe they were told to do as they were told. Who knew what really went on?

Sophie kept all the family informed of what funeral arrangements she could discover, mainly by dealing direct with the funeral directors. The actual information about the funeral from her brother fitted two lines of script telling her of a simple ceremony, one limousine and that flowers from immediate family members only! Very succinct. Her own first-class stamp that she had given to Hannah so that she could write a letter to Sophie and get a neighbour to post for her had been used. The post stamp was dated on the 18th received on the 19th and the funeral was on the 23rd. She could only assume that it had been hoped that the note would not arrive in time to give the information to the people wanting to attend the congregation, some 40 people! Everyone was there to greet Hannah when she arrived. It was obviously a very sad day for her. Sophie noticed that the new clothes that she had bought for Hannah which would have fitted her and kept her warm were not worn. Her poor mother had on clothes more suitable for Summer and she was shivering! Sophie gritted her teeth and decided that come what may she was not going to be goaded into a reaction, even when her sister-in-law gave her a shove in the Chapel she did not react. In fact, Sophie spoke to everyone, even her brother. Only common courtesies maybe but at least she was not going to be accused of irreverent behaviour!

So much of the service was a sham. Family names were wrong or pronounced wrongly; it was all rushed through as if there was a train to catch and no refreshments for the mourners. Nobody expects a three-course meal but, as a courtesy to those who have travelled some distance, and probably not had breakfast, it is customary to offer some tea, biscuits and a toilet! Sophie's brother's family had booked themselves in for a full meal at a restaurant. She supposed that she was to be grateful that they at least took Hannah with them for the meal! She later found out that Hannah ended up paying for that meal and many others that followed!

The rest of the mourners found a local pub for a quick meal and raise a glass to Randall. Poor Dad, thought Sophie, he would have been mortified that his sister wasn't even asked to attend the restaurant and had been treated in such a shabby way. He was so fond of this sister and so close. He must have been doing somersaults in the sky!

During the weeks that followed Sophie and John visited Hannah to make sure she was okay and that she had all that she needed. This was essential to Sophie as she now was not at all convinced that Hannah was being looked after properly. By the time Christmas was almost upon them the flat had been tidied and Hannah had come to terms with losing Randall. Sophie quizzed Hannah about what she was going to do for Christmas; did she want to go to hers for Christmas day or the whole of Christmas. "No," said Hannah, as her son lived just around the corner she would be going to his.

So Sophie and John took her card and present down to her and told her to phone them if she decided to change her mind. Sophie phoned Hannah Christmas eve morning so that she didn't interfere with whatever her brother was planning for Hannah. She and John wished her well and reminded her that if she changed her mind there was no problem they would quickly come down and get her.

Christmas passed without reaching Hannah on the day. She had said she was having a family meal with Sophie's brother so Sophie didn't think that anything was amiss.

During the following weeks Sophie got a phone call from her aunt (her father's sister) telling her that Hannah hadn't been taken for a meal on Christmas day and had, as she repeated "had just a sandwich and gone from room to room crying and kept looking out of the window, all dressed, waiting to be picked up"! Sophie got a similar phone call from her mother's sister and her husband telling her that they had received a telephone call saying the same thing.

Sophie and John went down to Hannah's to find out what was going on, they'd only been down the day before and Hannah hadn't mentioned it and Sophie had also sent a letter asking about her Christmas, without any mention. When tackled on what really happened over Christmas the truth came out: yes she had only had a sandwich for Christmas day, yes she had gone from room to room crying because it had gotten late and dark and still nobody came for her! she went on Boxing Day for a meal and then was brought home. "Why on earth didn't you ring us, Mum, and we would have come down and collected you!" Hannah said she didn't dare because she was frightened that Sophie would have gone to her brother's and asked lots of questions and made a scene. "Too bloody right," Sophie said. Hannah said she'd been told she couldn't go Christmas Day for a meal because they always had another old lady go there every year. "Do you mean to say that they couldn't have had you both there together, somebody for you to chat to of your own age?" "After losing Dad John and I would have had you with us all over the Christmas period and New Year"! Sophie said.

At this point, she could see that Hannah was looking upset and tired and decided to let the whole thing drop. Hannah asked Sophie not to say anything to her brother in case it caused trouble for her. Sophie said she wouldn't but this last statement was the last straw. What was Hannah worried about? When Sophie discussed this with her cousin she reminded her that Hannah was all alone in an environment she didn't know and was totally reliant on her son and his wife and sons to see to her shopping, her prescriptions and well-being. Sophie reflected on what her cousin had said and decided not to do what her instincts told her but to just keep in regular touch with Hannah and see how things panned out. It was a good job she did because before long there was to be yet another incident which was going to push Sophie's patience to its limits.

It was some little while later that Sophie and John took her cousin to visit Hannah. Whilst there the post turned up and John handed it to Hannah. She tried to open the letter but her arthritis meant she was fumbling to do so. John asked her if she wanted him to open the letter for her and she said yes. It turned out to be a financial statement. Whilst opening it up and giving it to Hannah John noticed that more than £6,000 had been taken out of the account and he quietly brought this to Sophie's attention whilst Hannah was looking at it. Sophie's cousin intervened here and asked Hannah if she needed anything explained to her or needed help with checking the statement. Hannah said that she didn't really understand the statement and that she left all that sort of thing to her son and usually put all the posts together, in a pile, on the table, for him to take home with him to deal with. This sent alarm bells ringing for Sophie's cousin. Both she and Sophie had spoken on many occasions about Randall's sister's visit when she couldn't find him (she never did get to say goodbye to her brother) and Randall's conversation in the hospital. She tried to explain the statement to Hannah and asked her why had so much money gone out of the account.

Hannah seemed to think that it was for the upkeep of her bungalow, rent for the flat and her shopping and heating.

Bit by bit Hannah was shown that shopping was clearly bought on a card and that £6,000 was a lot of money to go out in a month. She was shown what was her rent that came out every week and that, also, £2,000 in cash was taken out. What was it for? Hannah began to panic now. Did she have any money left? Was she destitute, she remembered Randall had tried to tell her one night about £5,000 being asked for and, as he had a loud voice, she was worried that all the neighbours would hear him and told him to tell her in the morning instead. The one time she should have listened to him she was more worried about the neighbours listening to their private conversation. Sophie's cousin asked Hannah if Sophie could take the Statement home to look over for her. Hannah said yes, she had nothing to hide, and so the three departed on their journey home with lots to say about events and the possibilities of what was going on.

Over and over again they kept looking at what they actually knew had happened over the last year since Randall's fall and what they suspected. Little things kept popping into Sophie's mind, her cousin reminded her of what Sophie had said in the past was a bit strange and John, absolutely furious about the treatment of Randall and Hannah, added what he knew and what he had seen and what he had been told. What about that email that Sophie had received?

Prior to the move but after Randall's head injury, and Sophie's brother's first initial abusive outburst, during Sophie's regular emails with her brother he had asked about whether Randall and Hannah had made a suicide pact! Sophie told him emphatically no! Looking back on this insinuation it began to make Sophie wonder if a pattern had begun to emerge of what was to come. Never in a million years would her parents have contemplated such a thing. They had, at the time of one of their own parent's deaths mentioned that the other parent might not be long behind the first due to the standard of life that they had. Her father was the sort of person who had panic attacks in later life and never wanted to know about negative influences because of the effect they had on him and as for Hannah, she was inclined to revert to religion at times of stress and so would never have contemplated the taking of her own life. That would have been blasphemy to her!

Also, Randall's health and care were good whilst in his own home and under his own doctors and hospital. Four months in a flat without support soon put an end to his life and left his wife not only without her husband of over 68 years but her carer and support in her everyday life. Whilst together they were strong, separated they were like fish without water! Medical notes showed that Randall was not expected to die when he did. Certification had to be delayed whilst two doctors were required to deliver the Death Certificate!

Sophie said to Hannah about coming to stay with them for a little holiday. She agreed and said she would get a holdall ready with a few of her clothes and Sophie reminded her to put her medication in as well. They promised to come and collect her the next day when she's had time to pack. But, later that night Sophie got a phone call from Hannah that she couldn't come because she had a headache. This happened twice!

Sophie's brother had arrived and seen the holdall and forbade Hannah to go and spend time with Sophie. There was obviously a lot of pressure being put on Hannah and Sophie wasn't happy about this. It was time to make sure that others were going into the flat to check on Hannah and make sure she was safe, happy and well and not being abused.

Chapter 7

Sophie and John continued to visit Hannah on a regular basis but one day, not the usual day to visit, they both decided to pop down to see her. When they arrived they found a neighbour with her. "Thank goodness you're here," she said. Your mother just keeps saying that she's not safe and she can't stay here"! Sophie thanked the neighbour for her help and tried to find out from Hannah why she wasn't safe. She just kept rocking backwards and forwards saying she wasn't safe and couldn't stay there. Eventually, Hannah settled enough to explain that two men had gotten into the flat the day before and stolen her purse. Why was she left on her own, why hadn't Sophie's brother taken her home to his for safety? Bit by bit Sophie and John were able to understand what had happened. Two men had gained entry to the flat on the rouse that the cooker wasn't working properly and that they had been sent to put it right. One kept Hannah talking whilst the other walked around the flat, supposedly checking things for her, and then the two said all was well and left. After they had left Hannah had gone looking for her purse and found that it had been taken. She had phoned her son and a police car turned up outside her flat. However, when her son eventually arrived he told the police that his mother had made a mistake so they left. (It turned out he had said that Hannah was elderly and had dementia and didn't know what she was talking about). When Sophie later thought about this she was of the opinion that he didn't really want the police looking too deeply into things; they may have started looking into the accounts too soon!

It was obvious that Hannah couldn't stay on her own in this flat in her frightened state so Sophie and John spoke to an administrator who turned up on site and she suggested they took her back to theirs for a holiday. This was exactly what Sophie had said to Hannah. What a stroke of luck that the administrator turned up when she did. This meant that they were aware, but were they really aware of ALL that had been going on? Sophie decided not to ask too many questions but, instead, get Hannah out of there for her safekeeping and peace of mind!

As soon as they got home Sophie put the kettle on for a cuppa and sat Hannah in the lounge and chatted to her whilst John put the bed up in the study. Hannah started to relax and kept saying, "Thank you for letting me stay with you. I am so glad to be away from that flat!" Sophie told Hannah that she was going to put the phone on to speakerphone so that she could hear what was being said. Sophie phoned her brother and told him that she and John had brought their mother home to theirs and that she was not a missing person, she hadn't been abducted. This was important, as she certainly didn't want the feeling she had about her parents being "missing" aimed at her! She explained that the neighbour had said Hannah was traumatised and that she said she didn't feel safe in the flat. She asked her brother if he would like to speak to his mother and his response was an emphatic "NO"! Sophie felt really bad for her mother because she was listening to all that was said. Sophie said she would phone her brother again on the next day when she had found out more from Hannah as to what had been happening. Sophie would have loved to have been a fly on the wall after this call if she had known what his reactions were going to be the next day!

Sophie telephoned her brother the following day. He was very curt with her but, not deterred, Sophie went on to explain that "I think we've found out what's been going on" and with that he hit the roof and became so abusive that Sophie couldn't quite make out every word. She did make out the "f" word being used most prolifically! It appeared that what her brother had thought she meant was that she had found out all that he and his wife had been doing. In fact, Sophie was referring to the break-in and Hannah's purse being taken and how Hannah had been traumatised by this event and fearful for her life. It was all just so much happening to her in such a short space of time: Randall's fall, the move from their beloved bungalow, the tiny flat, Randall's constant in and out of hospital close to this new residence, his death, her isolation. It was a wonder that Hannah's health wasn't in a more precarious state.

Hannah became very tearful and started walking about the lounge. She had heard her son's rantings and ravings. She probably couldn't hear all the words properly, Sophie couldn't either, but she was able to hear the vehemence in his voice. Eventually Hannah stood still at the side of the chair she had been sitting in and looked down to the floor. Then she started to walk backwards. "No, Mum, no, you're walking back into the wall, you'll hit your head"! Hannah didn't seem to hear, Sophie took her arms so that she couldn't go backwards enough to hit her head. At this point Hannah starting hitting out and saying, "Get your hands off me, get your hands off me!"

"Mum, Mum, what's the matter? I wouldn't hurt you, you know that," said Sophie. John looked on in total disbelief. Sophie got Hannah to sit down and quietly started to talk to her to find out why this sudden outburst. "Mum, has anyone ever hit you?" Hannah didn't answer. Sophie tried again, "Mum, has any family member ever hit you or threatened you?"

Eventually Hannah replied, "Not hit me but well she said I had to sign some papers because she was entitled to 70%."

"70% of what, Mum?"

"She said I had to sign as she was entitled to 70%." By this time Hannah was looking very drained and Sophie decided not to ask any more questions. This she would have to do over a period of time. The most important thing now, especially after this last retort, was to get Hannah to her banking provider and get help and advice from them.

Sophie explained to Hannah that it was important to go and see what state the accounts were in, especially after what Randall had said in hospital about wanting to know where all his money had gone. She didn't want to worry Hannah but Sophie was well aware of the implications of fraud and, more importantly, the mental torment that it could create. First things first, banking provider, then a discussion with Hannah about what she wanted to happen and then take it from there. One thing at a time so that Hannah wasn't overwhelmed by it all. It all had to be explained to Hannah in simple terms. She wasn't an educated woman, she was of a different era and her family background meant that she would have left everything to Randall to do. Hadn't it been fortuitous for certain people that Randall had had such a bad head injury and had been persuaded to sign documents for his son to take sole charge!

Sophie and Hannah went to town and asked to see the manager of where Hannah's accounts were held. Briefly, Sophie explained what she had been told by Randall and that he had now passed on, and then what her suspicions were. The manager was absolutely brilliant. He listened, without saying too much and was very friendly to Hannah and asking her directly about certain things. Sufficient paperwork was produced to allow the manager to run a series of checks to identify all those involved in Randall and Hannah's accounts. With dates of when Randall had his head injury, their move into the flat and then Randall's death, which wasn't actually recorded, which it should have been, the manager checked the account and was able to produce copies. He said he could clearly see that transactions had been taking place, which were not normal transactions that one would expect of elderly people. He even showed dates of transactions of when Randall was seriously ill in hospital. It was at this point that Sophie broke down. No wonder Randall was distraught and didn't live long after the move and spent most of his time in hospital. Had it all been one big plan to get Randall out of the way so that Hannah could be persuaded to sign cheques and documents to allow vast sums of money to be withdrawn. Sophie couldn't explain too much to the manager because she didn't want to upset Hannah, she had been through enough already. The manager was able to show how a cheque for £50,000 had been presented for withdrawal and had been returned because it could not be sanctioned as it was thought to be fraudulent. It was presented again, and again, it was returned unsanctioned. He could then identify that the £50,000 was then broken down into five £10,000 cheques and on these cheques it had been sanctioned. If he had seen such cheques he would have asked lots of questions. He also went on to explain that monies had also been taken out of ISA's by electronic means that had not been sanctioned and he had no idea how they had managed to withdraw from these ISA's. It was agreed that the manager would look, with another colleague, into Randall and Hannah's accounts and get copies of statements and cheques.

Sophie took her mother home to theirs and bit by bit explained what the manager had said and meant and asked Hannah what she wanted her and John to do. Hannah said she wanted all her money put back and her bungalow. Sophie had to explain that the bungalow was most definitely sold and she couldn't return to it. Also, depending on what money was left, it was probably not possible to buy another property. The look on Hannah's face said it all. At this point Sophie thought it necessary to explain that Hannah wasn't destitute and for how ever long and, if she wanted, she could live with her and John. This seemed to brighten Hannah up a little but, from time to time, Sophie could see that Hannah was going over and over again in her mind all the events of what had been happening to her because now and again she needed Sophieto confirm certain things and ask what if this and what if that. It was so much for Hannah to take in; she had never ever had to be involved in any money matters in her life. Randall did everything, all that Hannah had to do was keephouse, look after the children, get a little shopping and havea little cash in her purse for the milkman every Friday and save every week for when the coalman came. Her life wasalways a simple one, no high dramas, no extravagancies. Every item in her home had always been saved up for and been paid outright. Any worries Randall had coped with and now, with him gone, she obviously felt very alone, bewildered by all that had happened. Sophie and John justkept telling her that she had nothing to worry about and thatthey would look after her or, if she wanted, take her back to her flat (they hoped she wouldn't ask for that but, if shedid, well it was her life) or if there was anything else she wanted to happen they would do their utmost to make it happen.

As days turned into weeks Sophie tried to extract from Hannah whether she wanted to return to her flat around the corner from her son. "Absolutely not!" she had said. It was a relief and it enabled Sophie and John to look at what all the options were for Hannah. When they had first brought her to theirs they had turned the little study into a bedroom for her. It was small and without a wardrobe. Quite frankly there was no space for one, only sets of draws. It didn't even seem to bother Hannah. This was a surprise as Hannah was a very precise person and everything had to be exact and put away and no clutter! When discussing this with Randall's sister she pointed out that at Hannah's age and with all that had happened she would have just wanted to be safe and secure and know that she was loved. On reflection, Sophie could see what her aunt was saying. This facilitation for Hannah went on for some eight to nine months before she wanted a place of her own, albeit, only rented.

Sophie and John watched Hannah get stronger and took her out to buy her new clothes that were in keeping with the style that she used to wear. Hannah and Randall had both been very smart in their appearance and, although not that rich, always made sure that their home and themselves reflected their pride in themselves and their home and furnishings. It was nice to see that Hannah was beginning to be more of her old self. It was just such a shame that Randall was not there to be with her. Lots of outings were called for to help Hannah's well-being. All the old haunts that she and Randall used to frequent. Also, of course, she had her sister-in-law and niece close by and could visit them whenever she wanted. It was necessary to get Hannah strong so that she could face whatever might come next. It just seemed strange that every time Hannah was taken out she wanted to pay £60 for the petrol! When asked why to pay for a joint outing when Sophie and John wanted to go out anyway she explained that £60 was what she always paid out to Sophie's brother and his family. As you can imagine Sophie saw red at this. What a cheek to ask one's parents to pay for an outing that everyone was going to. Yes, Hannah had said, she always paid and she used to take them out for meals to a restaurant and also paid for the carpet to be vacuumed, £40 was the asking price! When Sophie later checked the bank statements she could see that yes, Hannah had paid and, in fact, even when she was not in attendance. Also, she had actually paid for her own special birthday meal! Sophie pointed out that it was usual for children to treat their parents to meals out and especially for birthday meals out at a restaurant!

The local police had been approached about what had happened to Hannah and the police from the area where she had lived in the flat called up and questioned her about the two men who had burgled her. Sophie had to point out that these burglars only took a pittance of what her brother had stolen from his father and mother. This officer drove up to see

Hannah on three separate occasions and on each visit took three hours of talking and each time her sergeant called her to find out where she was. The last visit this officer tried to say that Hannah was old and didn't know what she was talking about but, when Sophie had to leave the room to go to the toilet, this officer had gotten Hannah, who was supposedly so far diminished in responsibility, to sign a statement. What she had gotten her to sign Sophie didn't know and all that Hannah could tell Sophie was that the officer turned over pages and got her to sign the last page and told Hannah she would fill in the rest! What did that mean? When asked about what was to happen next Sophie was told that no further action would be taken. Strange!

Hannah's family solicitor was asked to visit her at Sophie's house to discuss all that had been going on. It was explained to him that Hannah was now living with Sophie and John for safety. He was absolutely brilliant! He put Hannah's mind at rest about the things that could be done and also what might not be so easily achieved. First of all, he had said, was, because of what the police officer had said to Sophie, in front of Hannah we might add, that doctors would need to give an evaluation of mental ability. This was a special test, recognised very specifically in law. It looked at understanding and being able to make decisions. Once this had been undertaken and confirmed, then it was of paramount importance that a Will be made and also Power of Attorney. This would allow Hannah to still be in control of herself and her assets and, with Sophie's assistance, she could if and when necessary, let Sophie make decisions for her. This was undertaken and achieved. Also, the solicitor would look into the fraud and see what was practically achievable and what was not. This way all evidence would be available to him to use as necessary.

Chapter 8

Sophie now spent most of her time making sure that Hannah was not only fed and clothed as she should but also that all those necessary appointments like the opticians, the dentist (Hannah only agreed to go once!), the hearing aid centre and her regular doctor's appointments to check her heart and medication and her general well being. Up-to-date hospital checks were made too for an X-ray of her lungs and scans of her heart to make sure all was okay. Thankfully there was no change. Bit by bit Hannah looked better physically and mentally. She kept asking questions and Sophie answered them all truthfully. Now was not the time to keep Hannah in the dark as others had done, it would serve no purpose. Every time a bank statement arrived she would sit down with Hannah to explain what had been spent, the receipts to go with it, the running totals listed by hand and then itemised on the new statements that came in. Hannah understood this, vaguely, Randall used to do the same but she used to leave him with the sole charge of organising "all the bills and things!" Hannah was becoming more interested in the accounts. This was good. Sophie could explain in easy terms so that there was no room for misconception. It was vitally important that Hannah could see exactly what Sophie was doing and understand it and be aware of what had been spent and clearly for the sole use of Hannah. The only time this varied was when, after nearly nine months, Hannah said she wanted a place of her own. This was organised but, naturally, paints were needed, some new furnishings and extra little pieces of furniture. The furniture from the bungalow had been sold by Sophie's brother and wife and some of their old furniture was put into the flat they had organised for Randall and Hannah.

When Hannah had moved in with Sophie and John it had been seen as a holiday a break away. When Hannah had said she wouldn't go back to the flat around the coner from her son because she didn't feel safe then it was appropriate to close that flat and put what little furniture there into storage. Something else that poor Hannah had to pay for but, thankfully, a place was found by her niece which only charged nominal amounts and this was much more practical than selling and buying all new.

It wasn't easy finding an appropriate flat for Hannah. So difficult when someone has had their own property and is looking for similar but rented one and, also, at a price that would fit the "new" pocket that she had been left with. Eventually, a lovely little flat was found where Hannah could feel safe. Much bigger than the flat her son and daughter-in-law had found for her and Randall and much brighter. Sophie wasn't really convinced that this was a good idea because Hannah would still need them to help her with shopping. Hannah hadn't shopped on her own for years and in an unfamiliar area would find it difficult, not to mention that she hadn't travelled on a bus for years either. No, Sophie and John would have to pick her up and take her shopping and still keep up with regular trips out. Sophie explained to Hannah's new neighbours about the difficulties she had experienced and they were brilliant! They used to chat with her at every opportunity. A little difficult because Hannah was a very private person and didn't like others knowing all her "business" as she put it. In this instance, Sophie explained that the neighbours would be like the ones she had when she lived at the bungalow and would look out for her. If she needed help she only needed to knock on their door. Sophie suggested that she spend the first couple of nights at the flat with Hannah. No, she wouldn't have that, she insisted that she could cope and would be getting used to where everything was and tidying up and putting things where she needed them and could easily find them. It made sense, of course, it did, but Sophie was still not sure. There had been too many changes for Hannah between the ages of 89 and 91. Sophie couldn't interfere, it was her mother's life and she knew of old that her mother loved housework and would relish making everything spick and span. Even if it didn't need it!

The first night at the flat did not quite go to plan. The telephone company had phoned to make sure that the line was working properly. Hannah didn't have her hearing aid in and couldn't make out what they were saying. She panicked, thought her son had found out where she was and was trying to get her to go back to the flat near theirs.

Sophie got a desperate call from Hannah's neighbour that she was "a bit uptight" about the phone call. Sophie and John got in the car and went straight around to Hannah's. Once it was explained to Hannah that it was the telephone company she settled down. Thank goodness that Hannah had the presence of mind to get her neighbour involved. This neighbour was to become a very good friend to Hannah. She was concerned that Hannah was so anxious about her son coming to find her and take her away. This was a very difficult conversation for Sophie to have with this neighbour. There was nothing for it but to explain all to her so that she could understand Hannah's alarm. Thankfully the rest of the week and months to come Hannah had grown in confidence about her new surroundings and still came to have Sunday lunches with Sophie and John and a couple of meals in the week too. Also, she went to tea to see her sister-in-law and niece and also her granddaughter and great-grandchildren.

As time marched on Hannah opened up more and more about things that had been happening whilst she and Randall had been moved away, out of their beloved bungalow and into that tiny flat that didn't even have a bathroom. There was a toilet crammed into one corner with a dirty shower in the opposite corner. The shower tray was used for storage because that was the only low-level space available that Hannah could use. The hand basin was just about enough space away from the door to be usable and again all around it was used for storage. Not at all what Hannah had been used to. A very clean and tidy woman had been reduced to tears over how she had been used and abused. Then came the list of events and monies used to pay for things like laundry because her daughter-in-law wouldn't do her washing for her and for "general cleaning". There was no washing machine installed in the flat or dishwasher like Hannah was used to using in her bungalow because of her arthritis. She and Randall had one wardrobe between them. In her bungalow there were wardrobes and storage spaces and a dressing table all around her bedroom in the bungalow. None of their Marks and

Spencer towels and flannels were around the flat only a cheap brand. Apart from the bedroom, there was one room used as both a kitchen and diner and lounge. This could only accommodate two armchairs and the TV must have been too close for them to see properly without giving a headache. The dining table and four chairs were fitted into such a small space that having breakfast and meals must have meant that they kept knocking themselves on walls and chair backs. It made Sophie fill up with tears on many occasions. No wonder Randall just gave up!

Where possible Sophie would try and talk about nice things to keep Hannah buoyant. Plans were made to visit Hannah's sister. Trips were made to visit nieces and outings to places that held fond memories of when Randall was alive.

All the while Sophie could see Randall's face emploring her to find out where all his money had gone! She loved her father dearly. Yes, he could be hard work sometimes but then, can't we all? Yes, he was a typical Union man and very strong in his attitude to work and management. There was another side to him that Sophie saw, a man who was used to struggling to make ends meet, a man who put his family first. He wasn't a man to say sorry easily but, once he thought a matter over, instead of saying sorry you were right, you might get him to tell you that he'd "been thinking and had an idea"! More often than not it was an "idea" that Sophie had proffered but that Randall couldn't readily admit being a good idea because a female had thought of it!

Their favourite days were Wednesdays when he and Sophie would go shopping around garden centres together. It wasn't Hannah's idea of fun and so she stayed home doing her housework. There were so many things that Randall and

Sophie shared that they enjoyed; gardening, reading, debating, politics, and so many things that Sophie would not be able to share with her dad anymore. When he died she couldn't even grieve properly for him because she had to be there for her mother, she couldn't get upset because she didn't want to upset her.

Now was the time to get on with gathering evidence for Mum's solicitor. Hannah's Building Society had sent her a letter telling her that they would manage her money for her. The letter clearly shows that she is in substantial credit. It read:

"Due to your current situation, we have passed your account to the Customer Priority team. They will now manage your account and work with you to agree on a suitable payment arrangement?" It could only mean that "they" had a debt to be paid. Paperwork later found suggests that loans were taken out and needed paying back (to do with business liquidation and the start-up of another business). This led Sophie to believe that the holiday lets abroad had been mortgaged to the hilt and the home her brother and his family were living in was also heavily re-mortgaged. Dad and Mum's money was to be used to get her brother and his wife out of a fix that they had created for themselves, and will always create for themselves, because of their hedonistic attitudes. Eventually, all the money would be reduced to just the state pension and attendance allowance so that it was easier to put Randall and Hannah into a care home for the state to look after in totality. What an end to two people who had always put family values at the top of their priority list!

The banking statements were showing all sorts of usage not associated with elderly people. There were the regular cheques going out on a monthly basis which, the manager had said, looked very much like the amount required for a mortgage, then the large sums of cash going out every week when shopping for food was done on the debit card, as were other items like meals out for four people, then seven people. The cash being withdrawn at a wide variety of sites away from the flat Randall and Hannah had been put in. Randall's car had been taken away from him by his son and given to a cleaner in his son's business, Randall was having extreme problems with walking and Hannah would not have walked anywhere, not even to the end of the turning. Anything going into the flat and out of would have been undertaken by others. Neither of them was familiar with the area enough to feel confident going out and the one time that Randall did he fell and ended up in the hospital. What was it Sophie's sister-in-law said, "He'd thrown himself into a bush!" This couldn't have been any ordinary bush because Randall's sister saw his back and said it was in a terrible mess. Why oh why didn't they phone Sophie and ask her to bring them both home?

This investigation had to be thorough and done with a clear head. Sophie would be put under a lot of pressure. Randall's sister was crying for blood! "You tell your mum she is strong and not to let your brother and his wife get away with all that money. That's my brother's money, he worked hard for that and it should be there for your mum not them!" Sophie agreed but, this had to be done properly and with clear legal ramifications and Hannah would not be able to answer questions in court because she didn't know what had been going on until Sophie told her and showed her the accounts and cheques and explained exactly what she was looking at. Hannah wasn't worldly; her son knew that and had used this knowledge against her. All had to be handled with kid gloves. Nothing needed to be done quickly. In fact, quite the opposite. Sophie was to go on and collect three large folders of evidence. It showed how poor Hannah had been a lamb to the slaughter.

As previously said, Hannah's Building Society sent her a letter telling her that they would manage her money for her and the letter clearly showed that she was in substantial credit so it could only mean that Sophie's brother had used Randall and Hannah's account as security for a loan. It was criminal! Paperwork later found suggests that loans were taken out and needed paying back (to do with business liquidation and the start-up of another business). This led Sophie to believe that the holiday lets abroad had been mortgaged to the hilt and the home they were living in was also heavily re-mortgaged. It suggested to Sophie that transactions were being put in place ready for Hannah to be put into a care home at the expense of the state! It was criminal!!! The local banking branch identified fraud and notified the Customer Priority Team. They were told that Sophie's brother had said that his sister was trying to take the money from his parent's account. The local branch was able to tell the Customer Priority Team that it was the person who was informer that was the culprit and told them where and what to look at which showed, quite clearly, that this was not the case and was in fact the brother!!! All Hannah kept saying was "how could he do this to me?

I am his mother not his stepmother"! Sophie pointed out that even a stepmother should not be used in such an appalling way! Hannah said she would phone her son and ask him why he had done what he had done. "I would have lent him money if he needed it!" "Would you have given him all your money,

Mum?" "Well no, not all my money. I will be needing it won't I?" "Then that's why he got you and Dad to sign Third Party papers to get access to all your money because he needed all of it and even that would not have been enough to pay off all his creditors. He couldn't sell his holidays lets because they would have been mortgaged and re-mortgaged to the hilt and the bank would not have lent him any more money. There was nowhere for him to go. He'd borrowed £10,000 from his wife and not been able to pay it back and she was pushing him to pay her. Perhaps that's why she said you had to sign paperwork so that she could get 70% of the money. She had probably been lending him money all along." Don't you remember, Mum, that you received a letter asking you to sign paperwork for them to take money out of your accounts at source to pay for, presumably, a loan against whatever had been put in place to siphon off money to get both his mortgages and businesses put in a better position!" Sophie was very, very angry but kept her cool so that she didn't upset Hannah.

Cheques had been going into different accounts and different names and even joint accounts with Hannah and her son with different banking providers which then after a short while were closed when money was transferred into yet another account with another banking provider. All were handwritten by the same person but with Hannah's signature. She had NEVER signed a cheque before in her life! She was so trusting, she hadn't thought that her son would have defrauded her and definitely not of so much money. To make it worse, he actually got the police to believe that his "mother wanted him to have all her money"! The police couldn't even take the time to do any checks with either the building society or banks or other family members.

Sophie made sure that Hannah had her telephone directory close at hand so that she could phone anyone at any time. Even her son, if she wished. Sophie only said to her mother to make sure if she did ring to pick a day when she felt strong just in case there was any altercation so that she could take it and that if it became "too heated" to "just hang up and put the phone down, Mum!"

Sophie encouraged Hannah to phone her sisters-in-law as much as possible and write letters and cards. This wasn't easy for her as her hands were very arthritic so at times Sophie would write for her. Hannah loved getting the post to read! She also loved her visits to her sister-in-law down the road. When her niece had garden parties the two ladies, in their nineties now, would sit huddled together laughing and giggling. It was what the pair of them needed, company, talking and laughing and, most definitely giggling. Mind you, the giggling was probably due to the "little" glasses of sherry the pair of them were partaking! Photos of the pair of them were to bring great joy in the years ahead. So nice to see two widowed ladies still clinging to life!

It was about this time that Sophie was feeling very, very low. She still hadn't had any opportunity to grieve for her father because she was too busy looking after Hannah and sorting through piles and piles of paperwork. Sophie couldn't talk through all that she knew with Hannah, it would have been too upsetting, she couldn't talk to John because he got upset to see her upset and it wasn't fair to discuss what she knew and show all the evidence to her daughter because she would have been upset to see her mother upset. Sophie decided to have a chat with her GP. She knew that if only she could talk through all that was going around and around in her head it would help. It wouldn't take away that lasting picture she had of Randall in the hospital when he asked her to find out where all his money had gone, but it would give her clarity and, perhaps, a decent night's sleep.

Unfortunately, there were no appointments to be had with anybody! Too many people were asking for referrals and not enough staff. "But doctor, I only need a couple of sessions to help clear my head and get some sort of perspective." Again, not have enough resources, but, she did get a telephone call from someone who gave her a telephone number to ring. "Don't be put off that it's a Counselling Service at a Church!"

Sophie made the call and went along for her first session. She wasn't sure what to expect and didn't really know how she was going to start the conversation. She had no need to feel anxious as the person she was introduced to was of a similar age and very}' friendly. Sophie explained that she didn't know where to start as so much had been happening to her, her parents, her father's demise, and her mother totally lost without him. Yes, there were a few tears to start but, after a while, she managed to explain all that had led her to seek someone to talk to who was not involved and could be objective. The counsellor explained that she would listen but not make a judgement.

The first session was mainly talking through what Sophie could expect from her session and that, normally, there is an expectation, that there would be quite a few sessions. In actual fact, Sophie only needed three. Yes, there was a charge, but she came to realise that it wasn't as important as she first thought. It was deemed money well spent!

At session two, Sophie was able to open up a lot more to

the counsellor and fully impart the trauma that had led to her father's death and how it had impacted on Hannah and to the level of support she needed. Before long, Sophie found herself feeling much more relaxed and the words just flew away from her. She was able to talk now without feeling upset. In fact, the counsellor commented, "I am amazed that you are in so much control and not showing anger!"

"Make no mistake," Sophie said, "I am very angry. In my mind, my brother murdered my father and left my mother without her husband, support and confidant. Being angry will not bring my father back and will certainly not help my mother and the rest of my family. They all need me and this is why I needed to voice all that I have pent up inside so that I can be there for all of them!"

At the end of the second session, the counsellor was asking questions which made Sophie feel that the counsellor had taken on board all that she had said. By the end of the third session, the counsellor asked whether the meetings had helped and what Sophie was going to do next. That was an easy one, first, make sure Hannah had all the help and support she needed. Second, try to make a better life for Hannah, even though it was without Randall and third, get all those papers into order so that the solicitor had one set and she the other, together with a spare set for passing on to others. It was necessary to get the word out to others to make sure that they didn't suffer as Randall and Hannah had suffered. However, the outrageous thing was that all those agencies that are put in place to help with housing, benefits and a whole host of other things, had all seen what had happened to Randall and Hannah many, many times before. Why on earth aren't these agencies feeding through the information they are picking up to government offices, especially Westminster so that the Law can do something about it?

Chapter 9

Whenever Sophie spoke to her relations their first words were always "what's your solicitor said, is he getting all that money back?" They really didn't get it. If they had taken the trouble to ask the right questions and listen when Sophie told them they would have had the bigger picture but, unfortunately, for them, everything revolved around money! They hadn't been the ones to see the effect that the move, the totally inappropriate flat, their home and all its possessions removed from them, and, yes, the loss of money which made them feel as if they were destitute. No amount of money would ever replace the loss of happiness that Randall and Hannah had been used to, the loss of feeling that "come what may" they would be together solving problems together and with loved ones. They were not used to isolation and coping with isolation. By the time any of us reach the late eighties we want our independence but we also expect support to enable us to have a modicum of self-respect and the respect of others that we try to keep to our routines, do most of the things that we used to do but with a little help and support. The more that is taken away from anyone and the more they are left in isolation means that they become forgetful, lose track of time and dates, lose interest in food, lose interest in communication, and too soon lose the will to live. What is the point of talking if people don't listen to you? None of these things relies on money alone, the prime motivator is the care and compassion one receives, the recognition that you are still worthwhile and have something to offer. Self-worth is an invaluable motivator to bring about health and happiness.

They didn't seem to get the fact that no amount of money would replace all the memories held in the bungalow for Randall, Hannah and for Sophie. The loft alone held all the artefacts that had adorned the walls of the London residence. The pictures that Sophie had drawn as a child, her paintings and her marquetry. All gone! Randall and Hannah had taken great delight in the fact that on their death Sophie and her brother would go through the loft and rekindle all the old memories. Well, that wasn't to happen now. The bungalow had been cleared of everything, even Sophie's things which had been held in storage at the bungalow, were all gone. They had either been sold for cash for creditors or had been given to "house clearance" or dumped! Nearly all of the family photos had been dispensed with into the rubbish tip or burned! Apparently, all evidence of the existence of family members and items of significant memory was destroyed. What sort of people would do this to over 100 years of ancestry?

Hannah was devastated that all these items could nolonger be passed on to grandchildren and great-grandchildren and, perhaps, even their children. Thankfully Randall and Hannah had allowed Sophie to take copies of some of the pictures but, unfortunately, not all. These older pictures weresupposed to have gone to qualified picture restorers.

All this got Hannah thinking more and more deeply about what she had lost. The next thing she was asking about was where was she to be placed at rest! "That's OK, Mum," Sophie said, "Don't worry I will ask the funeral directors"! What a can of worms this request opened up!

As Hannah had put it, she and Randall had been together since they were 17 and 19 years old, they had been married for over 68 years and were only ever apart during short hospital stays, otherwise, they were always together. Their wishes had always been that when they died they should be in their own bed at the bungalow and that they should be taken from the bungalow in their coffins to be cremated and placed in a double plot. This plot was to have a standard rose placed there with a brass plaque showing who they were.

In the absence of information being forthcoming from her brother about Randall's funeral Sophie had contacted the funeral directors direct for information to pass on to family members for the arrangements for the day. There were some 40 people who arrived to give Randall a good "send off". This thwarted the plans of Sophie's brother who only wanted himself and his wife and sons at the funeral with Hannah. He evidently had made it plain to the directors that they were not to discuss anything with his sister. As the manager put it, "Your brother is our client and paid for the funeral and plot so we cannot discuss anything with you!" The bank statements and cheques clearly showed that Mum had paid for Dad's funeral from their account and that on this account her brother most definitely did not have his name on the documentation. As far as Sophie was concerned Hannah was Randall's wife and their account had been paid so Hannah was their client.

With assistance from Hannah's longstanding family solicitor, Sophie managed to find out which solicitors her brother had used for some of his activities. She now approached them for information. They replied that they would forward a copy of her letter on to her brother. There followed a to-ing and fro-ing of information and this had the desired effect of a direct response from Sophie's brother. The letter started: "Dear Madam" – he couldn't even bring himself to write – "Dear Mum!" The rest of the letter, with attachments, carried on in an even further discourteous way saying that his mother must be suffering from dementia if she didn't know the arrangements for the funeral. He had all the paperwork so how would she know whether, in fact, their wishes had or were likely to be carried out to the letter? He went on to show letters that she was supposed to have written (very difficult as she didn't have a computer and, as Hannah's solicitor pointed out, these papers were not drawn up by a solicitor as they did not show any heading of solicitor's name, address, telephone number, or that they had been witnessed to make them legally binding). Poor Hannah had "no recollection of signing these letters and nor did she or would she say what was purported to be her words!" "Never, ever would I have said such dreadful things!"

Hannah was visibly distraught by the letter her son had sent her. It was just as well that she did not, at that time, know how much further her son was prepared to go. Sophie brushed it all aside and told Hannah not to worry and that she would sort something out. Sophie wasn't quite sure what at that time but with space to think she did come up with a few positive ideas. Firstly, if, by the time of events brought about by this vicious attack on Hannah, her ashes could not be placed with Randall what did she want to happen? Her Will was clear that in the event of her son not allowing her to be placed with her husband that her daughter was to place her where she thought

Hannah would have approved of This was an easy one. Somewhere bright and clean and with lots of flowers always! This still wasn't what Randall and Hannah's wishes had been. Sophie decided to try writing to her brother; naturally, she made sure she got the letter tracked by the post office so that he couldn't claim that he hadn't received it. That one had been tried before! As it happened his wife took acceptance of the letter and had been told off for doing so! This letter and others asked for clarifications on who was the solicitor that gave advice that Power of Attorney wasn't required and only needed Third Party, also to whom was this statement written and why it wasn't witnessed. As you may have gathered there was no reply to this letter! There were clearly signatures which changed from letter to letter and cheque to cheque. This didn't surprise Sophie as she had seen her brother's business documents some years earlier where he had gotten his mother to sign as Company Secretary in her maiden name. When Hannah was questioned about this she said her son had told her this would be all right. When Sophie had questioned whether she got paid as Company Secretary Hannah remarked that she didn't and that her son was going to give her salary to his son who, if memory served her right, was about ten years old at the time! Evidently, it was a ploy to evade both the taxman and maintenance for his son to his first wife!

Sophie just kept trying by as many methods as was humanly possible to try and comply with both Randall and Hannah's wishes. For a time all this ridiculous time wasting was put on hold but, in two and a half years' time, it couldn't be put on hold any longer.

For the time being Sophie had to settle down to practicalities and keeping Hannah buoyant. Also, there was still the procuring of tangible evidence. She kept looking at the files and every time she reviewed them she saw more and more of what had happened, had probably been happening and all the things, which really didn't add up. Even down to the registration of that pathetic little flat. Randall hadn't completed the paperwork or signed for it and neither had Hannah. How did that ever get past scrutiny? This reminded Sophie of a conversation she once overheard between her brother and a Greek official who had asked about a woman's name on a document.

"The name," he had said, "belongs to my mother, it is a family home!" He had denied the place was a "rental", "No it was a holiday home for the family!"

Sophie remembered looking on a technical site and saw references to banking, qualifications that had supposedly been attained, and positions of authority showing experience. What was all this? This was a clear misrepresentation of the truth.

In Sophie's mind, you should rise or fall on your own merits. You should also be recognised as being truthful, honest, with loyalty and integrity and able to show clearly what your attributes are by the work you do and not what a website says you can do! This all just reminded her of the time she was told about an insurance claim that was suggested to be worse than it was. There was also that car insurance which was addressed to a quiet suburb so that the insurance would be cheaper than it should have been. Or was it for cheapness? Perhaps it was for a vehicle that nobody was supposed to know anything about! Whatever way Sophie looked at the situation it just seemed to get worse and worse and Hannah kept asking questions about whether her son would go to prison. "I don't know, Mum," Sophie would say. "Well, he will deserve it if he does because he shouldn't have taken all my money" was all that Hannah added!

Sophie always had to consider what questions were worth asking Hannah and which ones might be likely to upset her. The one thing she didn't want was her mother to be taken seriously ill on her watch, especially as she was now living mainly on her own. Yes, Hannah liked it that way so that she could do whatever she wanted when she wanted but, obviously, this was a woman who had never, until her son had moved them away, been on her own. Randall had always been there and even when in hospital for his cancer or his pacemaker, she knew that he was coming home and she would not be spending more than a week on her own and sleeping on her own. When they were moved and Randall immediately kept going in and out of the hospital for weeks at a time she still knew that eventually, he would be coming home. Now she knew that nearly every night she would be on her own, apart from at Christmas and other such occasions when she stayed with Sophie.

Hannah had a habit of being quite controlled when it came to answering some questions. For instance, the time that the two men stole her purse. Sophie had asked if they had hit or assaulted her – the answer to this question may shed light on her extreme agitation when they had visited her the day after the event and when they had got her home to theirs and she was backing away towards the wall. A straightforward "no" was uttered and a clear outline of their ages, what they were wearing and so forth. Sophie was surprised that Hannah had decided that these two men must have been linked to either the window cleaner on contract with the Housing Association or their other contractors because they were wearing black "boiler suits" type overalls with a red motif, although Hannah couldn't identify what the motif was. She had said that one was looking at the oven whilst the other was talking to her and asked her to show him other electrical areas in other rooms. She said they were gone very quickly but when she checked her purse it had gone! With other observations it was a "yes" or "no" but when asked if her son or daughter-in-law were rough or abusive she became quite loud with saying no but that her daughter-in-law tried to force her to sign papers. When asked if she had signed she said she refused. Does this link up with questionable signatures and the remark about "70%"?

Sophie decided to change the subject and ask Hannah about her 90th birthday when she was living at the little flat near her son. There obviously hadn't been any invite from Sophie's brother for her and her family so she and John had taken down a birthday card and a big bouquet of flowers for Hannah. When Hannah phoned two weeks later these flowers were still going strong and Hannah was over the moon at their longevity! She told Sophie that she was expecting her to be at her birthday and Sophie had to explain that she hadn't been invited. "Well, I told your brother to invite you and your family, I was looking forward to seeing them and the great-grandchildren!" Hannah further explained why she was disappointed not to have seen them all. She was taken to a restaurant by her son and daughter-in-law and their sons and wives and partners/friends, and they all had a meal but they didn't hardly say two words to her. "They all sat at the other end of the table talking to each other"! Sophie really felt for her. A very special birthday, the first one without Randall, and she was left in isolation again! Sophie guessed that they hadn't even made sure she had her hearing aid in. Perhaps they didn't want her to have her hearing aid in, that way she couldn't hear what they were talking about!

When Sophie checked the bank statements again she found that Hannah had paid for her own birthday treat and hadn't even enjoyed it!

When John and Sophie took Randall and Hannah out for a meal they had paid nearly every time, except once when Randall said he was going to the toilet and paid on his way back to the table. He knew it was the only way he could get away with paying!

Little by little Hannah opened up about little things that had been said. Like, for instance, she wanted to send a birthday card to her sister but had rung Sophie to get a card for her and send it off because it had been said that Sophie's brother didn't have time to get it and that he had said "I am not retired"! This was obviously a slur against Sophie and John because Sophie had been medically retired and John had taken early retirement to look after Sophie, Randall and Hannah. Sophie couldn't understand why he couldn't have gotten a card for his mother when he got her shopping, they do, after all, have birthday cards at Tescos! When Sophie said to Hannah that she couldn't understand why her brother had made such a ridiculous remark she had said, "Well, there's history between you isn't there!" "What does that mean, Mum?" "What history?" Hannah said she didn't know. "You can't just make statements like that and not understand what you are saying or referring to Mum!" Sophie remembered her nephew saying the same thing to her when she thanked him for telling her that her father was dead and that it wasn't his place to have done that but his father (albeit that he didn't phone until the day after Randall died). All that Sophie could get out of Hannah wasthat sometimes her brother was jealous of her. "Why,Mum?"

"Well, that time when you got him a job he was presented to everybody as your brother and not presented in his own name!"

"Mum, that was something that I had no control over and besides, if someone had addressed me to staff as his sister and not by name I wouldn't have thought anything of it. At that time I would have felt proud and protected that I was recognised as his sister if the boot had been on the other foot!"

Time was now approaching Hannah's 91st birthday. A special meal for her with Sophie, John and the rest of the family was organised. They collected Hannah from her flat and were just about to get into the car when she turned and said "I don't feel too good, I think I am going to collapse"! Quickly John scooped her up into his arms and rushed her back to her flat and called for an ambulance. They were brilliant, they came quickly and did endless tests but, after all that, said that they felt she would be better in the hospital in case she took a turn for the worse. Scans were done in the hospital and they suspected a Transient Ischaemic Attack. Sophie tried to make light of what had happened and told Hannah that if she didn't like her pork roasts she only had to say and not make a drama out of it. As you can imagine, this brought lots of chuckles from Hannah. She was beginning to look brighter but, to be on the safe side, the hospital was going to keep her in overnight. Hannah was put on a ward and her granddaughter and her husband and children came in to give Hannah her cards, and presents and balloons and a big pink feather boa! They couldn't make out who was more pleased with all these adornments, Hannah, or the rest of the patients on the ward and the staff Hannah still got her birthday but, perhaps, not quite as she expected it. Now Sophie and John were going in not just daily but two or three times a day!

As the year moved on Hannah had a fall and spent another night in the hospital. Again she had all the tests and scans. She was looking a little frail and Sophie asked if, perhaps, it would be possible to have some early morning care go in to help Hannah. This was arranged and Hannah also had alarms set up to raise awareness if she was experiencing any problems. This year Christmas would be a simple meal at Sophie's so that Hannah could be taken home early so that she didn't get too tired. Hannah was okay but, of course, she was older and showing signs of her age now. Christmas came and went and the New Year, very quiet affairs. By the time January arrived Hannah had been taken to the hospital again after a fall. It appeared that her body salts were not as they should be and this made her collapse. The hospital changed her medication for her and increased fluid intake and sent her home. Sophie and John decided that Hannah now needed to be in accommodation that would offer her more help and support but only if and when she needed it. She was adamant that she wasn't going into a care home and, quite frankly, she didn't really need that. What she did need though was staff on site that could be called to help immediately. The HEARS service had been good and they came out to Hannah quickly when she needed it but, unfortunately, there was a time-lapse. She needed someone with her quickly and within two to five minutes.

Hannah's sister-in-law had been moved to an assisted living establishment just after Hannah's birthday. Hannah loved visiting her sister-in-law here because she had her own apartment, which was very large. It had a huge bedroom en-suite, a well- equipped kitchen and a beautiful lounge with views over the countryside. Sophie and John asked Hannah if she thought she might like it there. She wasn't sure to start with and, quite frankly, Sophie didn't know if they even had an apartment available for her but she said she would look into it. Unfortunately, Hannah had another ITA and this enabled the hospital social worker to get a lovely apartment for Hannah. Before she moved in John and Sophie gave the place a freshen up and new carpeting. The day that Hannah moved in she was supposed to be in her sister-in-laws apartment whilst all her furniture was moved in. On that day her sister-in-law was rushed to the hospital and Hannah had to wait a week before she could show her how she was settling into this apartment.

Sophie and John went around every day to see Hannah in her new apartment. Was she pleased with her apartment? Did she like the staff who worked there and her neighbours? There was a definite yes to this! "Do you know that the staff here look in on me every day and ask if there is anything that I need"! said Hannah. "If l say no, they just chat to me and then go and help some of the neighbours. There's a man here that has lost his leg and needs help and some of the ladies!" "Are you happy here, Mum?" Sophie asked. "Yes, it is just a pity that your dad isn't here with me. He would have loved all this and as for the views of the countryside and the gardens, he would have been in his element"! Sophie agreed and said that if they had said that they no longer wanted their bungalow and wanted more instant help she would have sorted these apartments out for them. "Well, I didn't know that the bungalow had been sold did I. I never wanted to leave my bungalow!"

As the months moved on everything was looking bright and Hannah was so, so pleased with her apartment. She even decided that she would go down to the restaurant twice a week for a meal. Such progress! Hannah would always say that she wanted to cook for herself but Sophie had bought her a couple of Marks and Spencers "Ready Meals" and she enjoyed these as they were so easy to cook.

Then one day Sophie received a call to say that her mother had collapsed. This was a shock, as she seemed to be doing really well. Hannah had to be taken to the hospital with a suspected heart attack. Sophie and John waited with Hannah whilst the doctors did all their tests. Yes, she'd had a heart attack and they would monitor her. Another night in the hospital for Hannah. All the other times she had wanted to rush home but this time, she seemed quite content to stay.

Sophie made sure that Hannah understood that the doctors had said she'd had a heart attack. When asked whether she was or had been in pain and was it very bad, Hannah said that no she wasn't in pain, she just felt a little strange. Sophie just couldn't believe it. When other people have described having a heart attack they have said the pain was terrible and that they clutched their chests because of it. Hannah had been so lucky not to be in any pain. Quite remarkable!

The doctors said that Hannah could go home after the physiotherapists had made sure Hannah was walking properly. She had at one time dragged her left leg a little and they wanted to make sure that this was not a long-term problem. Before long Sophie got the call to say that Hannah could go home. What a reliet1 She and John picked upHannah from the hospital and took her home to her apartment. Already they had asked the housing provider if Hannah could have checks on her early in the morning and during the night. This was all put into place before she got home.

Sophie waited to see if Hannah would do her usual and insisted that she could do everything on her own and didn't need anyone to keep checking on her. Surprisingly, she didn't. She seemed to accept that all that was required was someone to make sure that she hadn't had a fall and didn't need any help early in the morning and last thing at night and a quick look to make sure that she had managed to get into bed okay. For this purpose, there was already a key safe in place. Sophie and John could pick up shopping early in the morning and then go straight around to see Hannah and do the vacuuming and heavy work so that all Hannah had to do was a little dusting. She loved dusting all her pictures. Hannah could still be independent and make her own teas and coffees and do a little washing up. She could have one of the staff help her to the restaurant still or ask them to sort out a meal for her.

Staff reports were good. Hannah had always either been in bed or getting into bed when they had checked on her but had always been up washed and dressed and having her breakfast and meds when they arrived to see if she needed any help.

Things were going well and then Hannah had another minor attack. Staff called the ambulance straight away and then phoned Sophie to meet Hannah at the hospital.

John and Sophie got to the hospital before Hannah so they sat in the back bay of the hospital where the ambulances came in and waited anxiously. When the ambulance crew wheeled Hannah in she and they were laughing and chatting and Sophie and John just couldn't believe what they were seeing. Yes, she'd had another attack but again Hannah had no idea what was wrong as she wasn't in any pain 'just felt a bit funny!" She was like a cat with nine lives. How could she do so well and not even seem alarmed, anxious, or even quiet? Her colour was even good. Had the ambulance crew made a mistake? No, they hadn't this was yet another attack but, thankfully, she hadn't hit her head like in January!

Again, things were going really well for Hannah but, yet again, she had a really bad turn and the ambulance was called. This time she didn't look so well. If this was yet another heart attack this would be her third attack and since the first one, they were happening approximately every three to four weeks. Not good.

This time the doctors were concerned for Hannah. Again she wasn't in pain but she kept saying how very, very tired she felt and she looked very pale. She had always looked good for her age, her skin had always been very good and youthful looking but now she was beginning to look her age. Hannah was kept in for nearly a week for observation this time. The doctors did all their usual checks but, unlike before, they weren't too keen to let her home. They said that this time her kidneys were beginning to deteriorate quite quickly and she complained that her stomach was aching but it was in the liver area. Sophie asked Hannah if she wanted to go home to her apartment. "No" was her reply, "I don't think I am well enough"! But three days later, when Hannah's granddaughter visited her in the hospital she asked if she could put her in her pocket and take her home. This was unusual talk for Hannah. When Sophie visited her later in the day she asked if Hannah wanted to go home to her apartment. "Yes, please get me out of here!"

There was one really nice Irish doctor in the geriatric ward. Sophie told her what Hannah's request was. She promised to have a group chat with all the doctors concerned with Hannah's needs and get back to Sophie. Some of the doctors weren't very keen for Hannah to go home but it was agreed that a special hospital bed would be sent home to Hannah's apartment.

The bed arrived the day before Hannah and also specialist carers were supposedly put in place. The Irish doctor had said that with any elderly patient you never knew if they would make a full recovery or have a relapse and she was the only doctor who actually took the trouble to talk to Sophie. When Hannah arrived home the medication sent home with her was morphine by injection. The hospital got in a carer through their social worker team and they proved to be totally inadequate. They didn't recognise the specialist needs Hannah now had and Sophie had an argument with those who sanctioned them because they were no better than cleaners! They couldn't even communicate with Sophie properly, let alone Hannah! Sophie didn't know why she was so surprised. Hannah was beginning to have extreme pain and was getting weaker and weaker. She found it more and moredifficult to swallow. Through the staff at Hannah's apartment,Sophie was able to get The St Elizabeth Hospice Team in.They were brilliant! They didn't treat Hannah like a piece ofmeat, they spoke to her all the time they were helping her with washing, turning her in her bed, making her laugh and generally treating her as if she was their family member. Hannah was better with them than with the nurses at the hospital. When Sophie explained that Hannah couldn't hear without her hearing aid and that even then she struggled and that if they looked straight at Hannah when they spoke she would be able to lip-read the words she couldn't hear. They managed this really well. Believe it or not, Sophie had explained this to the nurses at the hospital and had words with a senior nurse who decided that she knew best and that she would bend down and shout as loud as she could into Hannah's ear to be heard. Foolish woman had to be told that all that did was send wind into Hannah's ear. Sophie had worked with the education of nurses and knew that in the past nurse training and been good. She couldn't believe that any of these hospital nurses that she had witnessed had ever had proper instruction!

Sophie and John were spending nearly all day with Hannah and noticed that she slept quite a lot now. They cleaned the apartment from top to bottom to make sure that they kept infection away. They were with Hannah when it was John's birthday. On Saturday they were laughing and chatting with Hannah, although Hannah's voice was now becoming very quiet. All the pictures around her bed were dusted and made sure that they were all facing her so that she didn't have to lift herself up too much to see them. Whilst seeing to Hannah's needs Sophie felt her hand grasp her wrist. "Am I seriously ill?" she asked. Sophie said that she was and that she hadn't helped herself by refusing to take her medication properly after her last attack and that as she wouldn't eat more than a Sparrow's mouthful, she had let herself get low.

Whether Hannah knew she was on her last evening Sophie didn't know. Hannah asked Sophie to tell John how much she appreciated all that he had done for her. "I don't have to tell him, Mum, he can hear you, he is only in the lounge." Sophie knew only too well that John was listening just the other side of the door. Hannah went on, "And I thank you for all you have done for me, I really do appreciate it and I love you!" Obviously, Sophie returned the sentiment. It seemed strange, she couldn't remember the last time her mother had ever said that to her. It was always just assumed.

John and Sophie kissed Hannah goodbye and reminded her that everything had been cleaned and disinfected as usual and that the Hospice Team would be coming in to see her within the hour. Sophie said that they would be back in the morning to see her and that when the Hospice Team were in again they would go over to their daughter's for a quick birthday meal so that the grandchildren could give John his birthday presents. That was the last time they saw Hannah alive. Within a few hours of being in bed, the phone went asking them to return to Hannah's apartment because the staff thought she may well have died. They asked if Sophie wanted them to phone the doctor and she said yes. John and Sophie rushed around to Hannah's apartment but thought she may well have passed because of her serene look, although she was still warm so she hadn't passed long.

Now they had to wait for the doctor to confirm the loss and for the funeral directors to look after Hannah. They now had to phone their daughter.

Chapter 10

Sophie let everyone know that Hannah has passed away! Solicitors who had passed on letters in the past were used again to inform her brother and his family. After all the abuse Sophie had received after Randall's fall from her brother and his wife and then again after the funeral of Randall and again when Hannah came for a holiday and ended up staying, she really didn't need to go down that road again! Also, at no time during the past two and a bit years had her brother contacted his mother by phone or by letter and nor did any of his family. The letter had been prepared earlier when Hannah had begun to have these regular attacks and so it was sent out post haste. Everyone was informed of Hannah's passing and the funeral arrangements.

Hannah had prepared her own funeral. She could have had a cheap coffin but no, she wanted one that would look nice for the ceremony, even though she was being cremated! A limousine was also paid for so that her son and his family could easily attend. Even without his contact, she still thought that he would attend her funeral to show his respects. The ceremony reflected Hannah's life and included her life with Randall and his earlier demise. They were now togetheragain! Nearly all those that attended Randall's funeral also attended

Hannah's. As you have probably guessed her son and his family didn't attend. Randall's sister had been having similar problems to Hannah with her heart but she managed the journey so that she could say her goodbyes.

The wake was at a beautiful hotel out in the countryside. It was a popular place for Randall and Hannah to visit for lunches, teas and coffees and had wonderful views over Constable countryside. There had been talk some five or six years earlier about the whole family going away to a place like this for the Christmas period. This was dismissed because of the fact that their son had other commitments over that particular holiday time. The hotel staff knew Randall and Hannah quite well as they had been frequent visitors and were only too pleased to be able to arrange a spectacular spread with wine, teas and coffees out on the paved area away from any guests. This area had tables and parasols and a grassed area, which led down to the outside swimming pool. Not cheap but it was definitely the style that Randall and Hannah would have wished for! Everyone that attended Hannah's funeral and wake had said that this venue was a fitting end to two devoted people. They all agreed that Sophie had given her mother a good "send off" and Randall's sister had said, "you have done yourself proud and nobody could have done anymore!" This sentiment seemed to be shared by them all and it made Sophie feel more relaxed about all of the events which had led up to this moment. Out of chaos had come some aspect of calm. Sophie and John and their family could now think about getting on with their lives. It would feel strange going and spending time without Hannah.

When they thought about it they had spent most of their twenty-eight years together with both Randall and Hannah's well-being in mind. They hadn't moved when they had wanted to because by that time Randall was having more and more hospital and doctor's appointments. Both he and Hannah needed them to get them from A to B and on time. This was no problem so long as they knew well in advance so that Sophie and John's medical appointments weren't on the same day. This was easily achieved by keeping their diaries up to date.

It was now time for Sophie to try and see what arrangements had actually been put in place about joint internment for Randall and Hannah being interred together. Sophie tried again to try and get some sort of understanding and as dealing directly with her brother was impossible she immediately, after her mother's passing, sent a letter post haste to the solicitor she had previously corresponded with. This would have been received the next day. Again they passed on letters! The letter, including a copy of Probate, was sent with reference to the understanding that a double plot existed and the assumption that there was a place for Hannah (it had now been some two and a half years since Randall's death). Sophie explained that as her brother and his family hadn't attended Hannah's funeral (and hadn't even spoken to Randall's family when they attended his funeral) she had made another assumption that they didn't want to see any of Randall's family or Hannah's and so that her brother and his family could show their respects to their mother and grandmother, she and the rest of the families would abstain from this internment. She went on to say that as the rest of the families had said their "goodbyes" did this solicitor think it a good gesture if she was to get Hannah's ashes down to the cemetery via a local funeral director so that "Mum" can be laid with Dad in the presence of her brother and his family? She went on to ask whether the anniversary date of Randall and Hannah's wedding would be an acceptable date to get the ashes down for.

The letter of request for clarity over the possibility of joint internment was sent nearly two months before the anniversary date. Sophie had a strong suspicion that some sort of farce was likely to take place and a stringing out of time so that the internment didn't take place. Sure enough, another abusive letter turned up a week before the due date. She imagined her brother thought that he hadn't left enough time for the ashes to be put to rest. Wrong! Sophie had already made tentative arrangements with the local crematorium where Hannah's funeral had taken place. It had been a difficult explanation to put forward to complete strangers about what might and probably might not take place. Could they accommodate me at late notice? Could they assist with getting the ashes down to an appropriate funeral director where Randall's plot was? Yes, they could! All Sophie could do now was wait and see whether she received any correspondence from either her brother or his solicitor.

The letter sent from her brother was addressed to "the wicked witch of the north". She was surprised that her brother's geographical knowledge wasn't that good. He had after all spent many years touring this country and others in his search for holiday lets. Sophie lived in the east and had done so for some forty-five years. It went on to say that the letter sent to the solicitors was being returned "with the greatest of pleasure" but that the solicitors it was sent to was not his but his mother's and so if Sophie wanted them to do something she should pay them for their services. Evidently a postage stamp was too expensive! Certainly, no solicitor's expertise was required to do that and so why this tirade about payment? There had not at any time been any problem over monies on John and Sophie's part. It went on to suggest that his sister was a "lazy fat**** who had sponged off the state for years"! This was news to Sophie but she read on. It then went into a great discourse about the "rest of us who work" and about him not blocking his mother's ashes going in with his father and that he had told the funeral directors so and that he had told them to "ensure you pay in advance for their services"! As he was the one who had money troubles Sophie was surprised at this comment. Both she and John only took on board what they could afford. The only debt that they had ever had was their mortgage, which was now paid in full and early when John retired; even all the work undertaken for Randall and Hannah's benefit had been paid up in full by them. This letter then went on to be totally disrespectful to Hannah because he went into a tirade about how he thought Hannah had made Randall's life "hell" and, in brackets, "just like you" whilst Randall was "alive" and that he thought she "may as well continue after his death"! It ended with him saying that he didn't want to hear from Sophie again unless it was to be told that she was "dead" and then he and the rest of the world could "celebrate"!

Sophie wasn't at all surprised by this letter. This was his way of again trying to get her to keep her distance and not find out too much. She knew only too well that this was a true reflection of her brother's attitude to others. The only surprise she had was that he would be so ruthless towards their parents, other people yes, but not his own parents! When she decided to read the letter again for a second time she noticed that it showed her that when others try to persuade her that everything is someone else's fault that they have tried to deny recognition of their own inadequacies; their own shortcomings. Attack was obviously their best form of defence. Very, very sad!

There was nothing left to do now but to go ahead with Hannah's internment. First, she had to contact the solicitors to whom she had written for help with breaching her brother's brick wall. She had to let them know what arrangements she was now making for Hannah's ashes, with the full address and anything else which would be pertinent for them, including a copy of the letter sent to her so that they knew that there was no other avenue for her to follow. Who knows what they thought about her brother's disgraceful attitude?

Hannah now had to let all those others that needed to know just what the internment arrangements were. Randall's sister was all for removing Randall's ashes so that he and Hannah could be together in the county they loved. Sophie had already discussed this possibility with Hannah before she became ill. Hannah thought it a sin to remove someone once they had been placed to rest. Sophie could understand this and so the plaque that was placed at Hannah's internment was to read both Randall and Hannah's names, with reference to Randall going before Hannah but that now they were both together again and at peace. Sophie took heart that they were both together again as soon as Hannah had passed her last breath.

The little service took place on their anniversary of them being wed and having the standard rose that they had both wanted. The rose is called "Peace". Most appropriate under the circumstances. The surrounding area of the plot has an array of little shrubs with complementing colours. Hannah always liked soft pinks and peaches and yellows so that is what she got. As for Randall, he just loved all flowers and colours and Sophie knew that she had completed her father's and mother's wishes in the best way she could. Now she could visit them and make sure that the grounds people were looking after the plot. This they most definitely did. The little area where Hannah's ashes were placed was a mass of roses, beautiful shrubs and a walkway laid out as a sundial. In fact, this area was always in sunshine. Something that Hannah must have appreciated as she was always a chilly mortal!

Now Sophie and John could have a little rest and start to get their lives back but, not before, they had looked at all the files that had accrued. These needed to be complete in case the solicitor needed to look at them and just in case the tax man ever came back looking to see who should have been paying tax on all that money that was taken out of Randall and Hannah's accounts. When this was done Sophie could put stickers on relevant bank statements and the solicitor's file to show where there were anomalies. Nice word anomaly, it covers all eventualities!

Sophie now made a list of what she knew had been done and what she believed to have been done and why. There were copies of her brother's two businesses which had failed listed in local newspapers. This long-standing business had gone into Liquidation, then the second business started up at Randall's demise and only lasted eighteen months, the same business with a slight variation. Now there was a third business started up. This was the worrying one because this one was dealing in financial matters and other peoples' money and not his own. Sophie felt sure that what had happened to her father and mother had happened once before. A couple of years before Randall and Hannah were moved away from their bungalow conversations had taken place which suggested to Sophie that another person had been removed from the property due to money being shared out. She couldn't prove it at that time and, quite frankly, it wasn't Sophie's concern but, now with all that had happened she began to wonder to what extent this particular incident had been the initial catalyst to what had happened to Randall and Hannah. Then there was this other person who had made various visits to her brother's house and wasn't allowed to be there when others were. Was this person being defrauded? This person was also elderly. Sophie wondered just how many there were now who were being defrauded.

Sophie sought advice from a Private Investigation Service. She gave them the basic information of what she knew, what she suspected and what she, on her own, had found out. They said they were surprised at what she had found out and all on her own. After going over again what she had found out they said that she had done a very thorough job and that the only thing they would have done was look very closely into her brother's accounts and those of his close family members. They told Sophie that she could be proud of herself for not giving up and going it alone after the police let her and her parents down. With all this said Sophie now had to make a family discussion about what to do next. She had to be sure that she did not put any of her family at risk or in harms way!

Chapter 11

Now had come the moment when Sophie would take stock and look at what she Had in clear undisputed evidence. She had to be absolutely certain that she had crossed her "t's" and dotted her "I's" and could be able to explain facts from supposition, and not rely on hearsay. She began by bringing out all her old diaries. These were to prove extremely useful. Sophie wondered why she hadn't done this before, the chain of events that had led up to those first fatal days, and others were all there. Also, the texts and emails were all there and able to show who said what and when. Together with these and correspondence with professionals, a clearer view could be seen of other peoples' thoughts and attitudes.

Firstly, look at years ago, i.e. the only times brother and his family visited, every Christmas Eve only, birthdays, probably for their presents. Rest of the time he came up on his own so that he could talk to Mum and Dad on his own. Nothing wrong in that unless, of course, done so that his wife didn't know what he was saying.

Consider the times he asked for help with his business and his vehicles because his wife was "bleeding" him "dry" as Randall regurgitated to Sophie!

Then the time he suggested to Randall and Hannah that

they take the Equity out of the bungalow so that they had some spare cash. Why? They had over £30,000 in savings, inheritance and regular pensions coming in together with Attendance Allowances. No need for extra cash as this would have affected their benefits and, in the future, any inheritance which would have been due would be liable to massive reductions and even a loss of inheritance. Must have been having problems again with his business. Did know that his property was on interest only and the others were linked to the business. Nobody in their right mind ever links their home to their business. There was talk about re- mortgaging properties. That means more problems in the wind!

Then the time that Randall decided to change his and Hannah's Wills. The initial Will left money to everybody, including unborn children. Then when it emerged that there were financial difficulties linked to the business: it was suggested that money was "flooding out of the coffers" by the daughter-in-law and the children and that their Wills had to be changed so that only their daughter and son could inherit. This meant that Sophie's daughter and her grandchildren would not be recognised in the Wills. Sophie was instructed to make sure that the inheritance was only to be split two ways and to hold back on signatures if it seemed likely that money would be diverted away from their son by his wife. This would not have been very palatable to Sophie but, in the interests of helping her brother, she would have withheld her signature from documents to enable him to get himself straight, even if it was to prove detrimental to her for the short-term, again this meant Sophie's daughter and grandchildren would be affected until Sophie got her share, if at all! When Randall and Hannah contacted their solicitor to change their Wills and passed a copy to Sophie and her brother. Sophie didn't think anything about this Will at the time but, perhaps, if her sister-in-law saw her brother's copy of this Will would she have made life difficult for him? Was this when all the clandestine visits started or before?

Sophie tried to get her head around events and tried to put them into some sort of chronological order so that she could check hard evidence against what she had witnessed and what she had been told.

When Randall died Sophie checked with Probate and the Office of Public Guardianship, as to whether a Will had been lodged with Probate, and was told that no it wasn't. She then checked whether Lasting Power of Attorney (LPA) was registered in her brother's name or anybody else's. She was told that no it wasn't and that it would be very unlikely that the youngest child would be required to register when an elder child was alive and that there would have to have been some exceptional reason to give permission to the youngest child. Also, if there were any suspicion of any financial risk that person would not be given LPA. This would be why Third Party was used because then there would not be anyone looking into transactions with a view to fraud. With his business being so precarious and Liquidation looming he would have been seen as a risk and had lots of people asking questions. He would not have wanted police or authorities looking into his financial arrangements and definitely not the Inland Revenue!

Sophie, on the other hand, had no problem with LPA as her financial history was as safe as houses, always had been and her rating was very high too. This she knew because she was forever being offered extra credit on her Credit Cards and her building society was also keen to lend her money, even when she didn't want it!

Sophie looked at the bank statements and all the cheques. Firstly, Randall had, previously, been the only person to write cheques as Hannah never got involved with anything other than using cash for food and that Randall had given her. Then she looked at the bank statements and the cheques written after their move into the flat. She even looked at the flat's tenancy agreement and who completed it and who had signed for it. A strong pattern emerged. It was the same handwriting! Cash, on a regular basis, was withdrawn at various cash points. Randall was in the hospital or sent home to be housebound only to end up being returned to the hospital in a very short space of time. None of his signatures showed at all. Hannah's signatures, some disputable, were shown on the cheques and some documents but, even when you looked at these signatures, they varied.

What did they signify? Hannah had said that she didn't even recognise her own signatures on cheques or what these cheques were used for. Again you came back to the fact that Hannah never ever got involved in anything financial and that she couldn't even write a cheque. The massive outgoings and cheques were depleting the accounts at an alarming rate at about the time just before Randall's death. Also, ISA's were being closed down and transferred elsewhere and not on Randall or Hannah's instructions. Why did the financial authorities involved never question so many transactions, such large sums and the regularity of large cash withdrawals with such frequency never undertaken by Randall before in all the time he had the accounts? Also, how was the ISAs manipulated via the internet or telephone calls? This was also something that Randall would never have done and had specifically set up NOT to happen. Why did nobody raise an alarm at the banks or building society? Are staff not trained to identify such anomalies?

Sophie now looked into newspapers and what, if anything was listed about businesses, and their owners or staff. This identified the liquidation of the business and meetings with creditors and dates. This proved to be very useful indeed!

Now Sophie had to look at historical data to see what had happened earlier. This is where she identified what looked to be fictitious names and also that at one time Hannah (not using her married surname but her maiden surname) was the Company Secretary, but received no money, and later her sister-in-law and other family members became Company Secretary and Directors. There were also messages from disgruntled ex-employees referring to cheap labour being taken on and references to them being supposed to be illegal immigrants!

Sophie looked again at the Tenancy Agreement to the flat that Randall and Hannah had been moved to. There is normally a declaration to be signed to say that you do not/have not ever had your own property. There was no reference to them owning their own property and what it had been sold for. Why did nobody pick up on this? Sophie knew of one person who had listened to Hannah about how she just wanted to get back to her lovely bungalow. That person was encouraged to leave the housing association. The person who took over her position was on very friendly terms with Sophie's brother and sister-in-law. She was right back again to the same two people linked to everything, including being linked to the first person she suspected of being manipulated the first time!

More and more Sophie could see just how important it was to show to others how easy it is to extract money and assets from the vulnerable. The many agencies that Sophie had contacted whilst dealing with Hannah's social and medical needs and also financial, had all said that they were well aware of very many cases where the elderly and vulnerable had been targeted as easy prey to withdraw money and assets from them. These agencies need to unite and solidify policies and information to each other to counter fraud and abuse. Recognition of the difficulties incurred by victims to be able to speak out on their own when it is likely that the perpetrators are the ones that are relatives and appear to be looking out for them. At no time should these elderly and vulnerable people be left without the support of those agencies put in place to protect them. There needs to be advocacy in place to protect them! There needs to be accountability!

Sophie was adamant that she must get the word out to other vulnerable people. If only one person is saved from suffering the same plight as her parents then it would be worth all the effort and the heartache of re-living the last harrowing years. Adversity is character forming. It is necessary to fight to survive to be able to be a good advocate for all those without a voice! What is required is courage, moral fibre and conviction. There is no room for revenge but justice must be sought. If a crime has been committed justice must be seen to be served.

Chapter 12

Sophie had completed Randall's task he had set her. She had found out where all his money had gone and looked after Hannah in the style to which she was accustomed and kept her happy. She had enabled Hannah to get back happiness for the remaining two years of her life!

Sophie felt that she couldn't express enough just how important it is to never under- estimate the need for taking copies of everything; you never know when you may need it. Even Sophie, used to administration and report writing, let valuable pieces of information slip through her fingers purely because she trusted those close to her and never would have believed she would need proof of absolutely everything because of deception and so-called professionals being blind to implausibility and being "sweet-talked" by others who look like professionals in suits and said the right words!

Sophie went on to collect emails, pictures, bank and building society statements, texts and voice messages, diaries and notes and wished she had listened to her inner voice more. If something doesn't seem right you can bet that it isn't! Our own natural instincts work well when we look at strangers but, unfortunately, more often than not it is those who are closest to us that let us down. One wonders how they would feel if they found themselves in the same boat when they get older! It is important to consider whether, in the light of what transpired with Randall and Hannah, whether Solicitors need to have a special holding bay for Wills, separate from their own offices, so that if anybody tries to use coercion through another Solicitor then a trusted body holding previous Wills can ask the right questions, especially where Third Party access to accounts is concerned. Most Solicitors would be cautious of cutting out beneficiaries and would expect to see detailed notes and information.

Also, Government Agencies need to ask questions when dealing with the elderly, the frail, and the vulnerable. There needs to be a proper checklist in place to verify that all monies are for the benefit of the expected recipient. Not just taken on one person's say-so!

Sophie's Check List will be:-

1. A Will that can't be manipulated. Named Solicitor (perhaps a family solicitor who knows very well if anything is amiss) that has to be involved with any transactions so that misdemeanours cannot occur.
2. Clear banking and building society statements which show what is the usual deposits, transfers and monies being taken out and perhaps a stipulation that any monies over £2,000 or £3,000 a month have to be verified and linked to the bank manager or solicitor. If not verified but money is still taken out then the manager or those monitoring transaction is responsible for the fraud has taken place.
3. Regular doctor visits to ascertain whether more stringent measures need to be put in place, i.e. not just

DNR (do not resuscitate) but also other advice like frailty of the mind and body. Being able to hear what is being said properly is a major factor with theelderly and their signatures.
4. Copies of documents to be put in a special bank or building society vault for managers/solicitors to refer to on death or very ill health.
5. Inland Revenue: perhaps the IR need to be more integrated with monetary organisations to make sure that there are no areas for concern.
6. Make a list of those who have to be involved in monetary transactions before any monies, cheques, or cash can be utilised by others and more stringent tests on signatures!

There is a big gap between Heaven and Hell. Most of us strive towards Heaven forever looking upwards always trying to do the right thing. Unfortunately, there are so many amongst us who seem to decide to go the other way constantly rushing towards Hell with the atrocities and the ridiculous ideas of what is their worth and what they are entitled to regardless of who they hurt along the way through sheer greed and a lack of moral fibre. They may seem as if they prosper, at first, but in time they all get their just desserts! Confession is good for the soul! Misdemeanours will not stay hidden forever and Justice will prevail.

Epitaph

In Sophie's words:-

"When one makes money their God and shows no love or humanity to anybody, let alone one's older vulnerable relatives who share the same blood, it is the lowest point anyone can reach. Money isn't needed to show love, respect, care and responsibility. Money isn't needed to have honour and integrity and be able to walk down the road with one's head held high and a clear conscience"!

Sophie felt she could meet her parents and ancestors on the other side when she passed over with a clear conscience.